I0766336

Screams Of The Mind And Echoes Of The Heart

Screams Of The Mind And Echoes Of The Heart

Amaan Shabir

Amaan Shabir

CONTENTS

CONTENTS

CONTENTS

Instagram Handle: @Amaanshabirofficial

Email: amaanshabir09876@outlook.com

Twitter Handle: @Amaanshabiroff

In the heart of a forgotten town, where shadows danced like spectres in the flickering lamplight, a sinister regime held sway. Under the iron grip of a corrupt figure of authority, the people suffered in silence, their cries drowned out by the echoes of oppression. Streets once bustling with life now lay barren, choked by the tendrils of fear and despair that gripped the populace.

At the centre of it all stood the enigmatic protagonist, a solitary figure amidst the chaos, his soul a battleground for the forces of light and darkness. Born into a world devoid of love and compassion, he navigated the treacherous waters of power and revenge with a heart heavy with longing. In a society where tyranny reigned supreme and pain was currency, he sought solace in the fleeting promise of love, only to be met with betrayal and despair.

As whispers of rebellion echoed through the cobblestone streets, the protagonist stood at a crossroads, his destiny intertwined with the fate of the town itself. With each step forward, he delved deeper into the abyss, grappling with the demons that threatened to consume him whole. And as the shadows lengthened and the night deepened, a sense of foreboding hung heavy in the air, heralding the arrival of a darkness that would test the very limits of his humanity.

In the darkness of the night, amidst the ruins of a broken society, the stage was set for a battle of epic proportions, where the line between hero and villain blurred and the true nature of power was laid bare. And as the first whispers of dawn broke through the horizon, the protagonist stood on the precipice of a new world, his fate uncertain, his resolve unyielding, and his heart yearning for redemption.

Echoes Of Solitude

In the heart of the bustling town, amidst the whispers of its forgotten alleys, lurked the loneliest soul. He stood as a monument to betrayal, his back adorned with a grotesque display of countless knives, each one a jagged reminder of his shattered trust. Blood oozed from the wounds, forming a macabre tapestry upon his skin, the crimson rivulets intertwining in a gruesome dance of agony. His smile, though forced, was a ghastly sight, like a mask of deceit barely concealing the anguish beneath. Alone in the darkness, he bore the weight of his solitude like a condemned man carrying his own cross, a solitary figure drowning in a sea of indifferent faces.

******

Take heed and grasp what you can from his pain-stricken existence. Do not hesitate to etch more wounds into his already burdened back, to cut his heartstrings with careless abandon. For this, my friend, is the way of society.

In a world where selfish ambition reigns supreme, where empathy is scarce and compassion a fleeting whisper, the loneliest soul serves as a stark reminder of our collective indifference. So, do not shy away from inflicting further agony upon him, for in his suffering lies the brutal truth of our existence.

Learn from his anguish, let it be your guide in navigating the treacherous waters of human interaction. Embrace the ruthless mantra that it is better to trample over others in pursuit of your desires than to extend a hand of kindness. For in this dog-eat-dog world, survival often demands such callousness.

So, take what you can from the loneliest soul. Let his pain fuel your ambition, his despair sharpen your resolve. And remember, in a society that values power above all else, sometimes it is necessary to sacrifice empathy at the altar of success.

A Shadow's departure

As I fade into the obscurity of the night, I can't help but feel the weight of my own impermanence pressing down upon me. Like a fragile leaf caught in a gust of wind, I am carried away by the currents of fate, destined to drift aimlessly in the vast expanse of time.

With each step I take, it's as if the blood from my wounds seeps back into my skin, staining it with the hues of my own despair. The scars that adorn my body serve as a constant reminder of my own failings, a testament to the pain that I have endured and inflicted upon others.

With every beat of my heart, I can feel the darkness creeping in, tainting it with the echoes of past mistakes and shattered dreams. It's as if my very essence has been tainted by the sorrow that courses through my veins, leaving me feeling like nothing more than a vessel for despair.

And as I fade into the darkness, I am acutely aware of the damage that I have caused, both to myself and to those around me. The blood that stains my skin serves as a grim reminder of the consequences of my actions, a constant reminder of the pain that I have wrought upon the world.

*****

I cast aside my own identity; it's all but a passing shadow. Observe as I silently evaporate into the ether, all in service of your well-being. In this transient existence, I may vanish like a wisp of smoke, leaving behind no trace of my presence. Envision me cradling you in the darkness, slipping away without a single whisper uttered.

This bed, adorned with borrowed linens and the lingering essence of another, acts as a vessel for my departure. I fade through the threshold, leaving no imprint upon the earth. You, like an oblivious bird, won't even sense the void I leave in my wake.

I might as well be a spectre, better suited to the shadows. So, I implore you, don't linger on my account. There's no fairy-tale ending to be found here. There's an undercurrent of impermanence, a feeling that my absence won't resonate. It's as if I'm merely borrowing space in this world, and now my time is drawing to a close.

Don't wait for me, don't linger for me. Pause, yet it's not a tale with a triumphant climax. I require time to navigate through my own labyrinth of turmoil, searching for threads that hold substance. There's a certain sense of futility in it all, yet there's an ache to be cradled in the depths of darkness. Nevertheless, I fear I'm bound for an unwanted destination, so don't wait for me.

Do not cling to the false hope of my return, for I am nothing but a broken vessel adrift in a sea of despair. There is no redemption to be found in my embrace, no solace to be gleaned from my presence. I am but a hollow shell, a shadow of my former self, and to wait for me would be to court disappointment and despair.

Take comfort instead in the arms of another, in the warmth of a love that knows no bounds. Find solace in the knowledge that you deserve better than what I can offer, better than the hollow promises and empty gestures that I am capable of. For I am but a wretched soul, a lost cause in the grand scheme of things, and to wait for me would be to deny yourself the chance at true happiness.

3

Betrayal In The Darkness

As I tread through the silent streets of the night, the world around me seems to hold its breath in anticipation of the dawn. The moon hangs low in the sky, casting a ghostly pallor over the landscape, while the stars twinkle like distant beacons, guiding me through the darkness.

The wind whispers through the alleyways, carrying with it the faint scent of rain and distant memories. It dances around me, a gentle caress against my skin, as if trying to soothe the ache that lingers within my soul. With each step I take, the sound of my footsteps echoes off the walls, a solitary rhythm in the symphony of the night.

The buildings loom tall and imposing, their shadows stretching out like fingers reaching for the sky. They stand as silent sentinels, guardians of secrets long forgotten, their windows dark and empty, devoid of life. The streets are deserted, saved for the occasional stray cat or lone wanderer, their presence fleeting in the stillness of the night.

Above me, the branches of the trees sway in the breeze, their leaves rustling softly like whispers in the wind. The air is cool and crisp, tinged with the promise of impending dawn. It fills my lungs with each breath, invigorating and cleansing, as if washing away the remnants of the past.

And as I continue on my journey through the night, I can't help but feel a sense of peace wash over me. For in the darkness, amidst the solitude of the night, I am free to roam unfettered by the expectations of the world. Here, in the quiet embrace of the night, I am nothing but a wanderer, a solitary figure lost in the vast expanse of eternity.

As I walk, enveloped in the eerie stillness of the night, a shiver runs down my spine, a premonition of impending doom. Without warning, I hear a faint rustling behind me, a sinister whisper in the darkness. Before I have time to react, a searing pain explodes in my back, as if a red-hot poker has been driven through my flesh.

I stagger forward, gasping for breath as blood gushes from the gaping wound, a crimson river cascading down my spine. The metallic tang of blood fills the air, thick and suffocating, as I struggle to comprehend the betrayal that has unfolded before me.

With trembling hands, I reach behind me, fingers sinking into the sticky mess of blood and flesh. I grasp the hilt of the knife, slick with my own blood, and pull it free with a sickening squelch. The pain is blinding, overwhelming, as I collapse to my knees, the world spinning around me in a dizzying whirl.

Through blurred vision, I catch a glimpse of my assailant, a shadowy figure looming in the darkness. Their face is hidden in the shadows, obscured by the veil of night, but their intent is clear. Another knife gleams in their hand, poised to strike once more, as they step forward with predatory grace.

I am defenseless, vulnerable, a lamb led to the slaughter. And as the darkness closes in around me, I am consumed by a sense of bitter resignation, knowing that this is not the end.

*****

In the vast theater of perception, I am the shadow that dances to the melody of your disdain, a ghostly figure weaving through the corridors of your consciousness. Each whispered reproach is a brushstroke, deftly wielded to craft me into the antagonist of your own narrative. You, the unwitting puppeteer, pull the strings of resentment, orchestrating a macabre ballet where I pirouette as the embodiment of your darkest fears, a specter haunting the halls of your mind.

Yet, amidst the swirling mists of your contempt, there lingers a subtle scent of betrayal, a bitter note that taints the very air we breathe. For in the quiet moments before the storm, there were whispers of trust, promises exchanged like sacred vows under the moon's watchful gaze. But now, those vows lie shattered at our feet, broken remnants of a bond once cherished.

As you cast me into the role of the villain, you sow seeds of bitterness, oblivious to the garden of discord that blooms in your wake. The mirror of condemnation reflects not just my visage but a distorted reflection of your own psyche, fractured and fragmented by the weight of your animosity. You stand at the crossroads, a weaver of enmity, yet blind to the fact that every strand you spin binds you tighter to the tapestry of your own creation, entangled in the web of your own making.

In this cosmic waltz, your hatred becomes the paint that colors my existence, staining me with the hues of your resentment. I am the canvas upon which you project your deepest insecurities, a living testament to the tumultuous landscapes within your soul. So, revel in the allegory of your resentment, for in this grand tale, you are both playwright and protagonist, sculpting a tragic narrative where the boundaries between creator and creation blur into a surreal dance of shadows, each step echoing with the rhythm of our intertwined destinies. And yet, beneath the surface of our twisted dance, lies the faint echo of betrayal, a haunting melody that lingers in the spaces between our silhouettes, a reminder of the trust we once shared, now lost to the winds of fate.

As I lay there, wounded and vulnerable, my gaze meets the eyes of the one who had delivered this final blow, and a wave of recognition washes over me. It is the very person from whom I had departed earlier, their visage twisted by a mixture of regret and desperation. In that fleeting moment of connection, I see the echoes of our shared history reflected in their eyes—the promises broken, the trust shattered, the bonds severed.

There is a profound irony in this reunion, amidst the chaos and agony of our present circumstance. It's as if fate itself has conspired to bring us together once more, to confront the consequences of our actions and the weight of our choices. In their gaze, I see the turmoil of conflicted emotions—the guilt of betrayal, the anguish of loss, the haunting spectre of what could have been.

4

Mirror Mirror

Within the silent chambers of my soul, where echoes of neglect reverberate endlessly, there exists no space for apologies. Like a solitary tree standing amidst a barren wasteland, I am but a forgotten monument to solitude, with no audience to receive my words of contrition.

Amidst the symphony of life, I am but a muted note, drowned out by the cacophony of indifference. The winds of apathy howl relentlessly, stripping away any semblance of connection or empathy, leaving me stranded in the desolation of my own existence.

Here, in this barren landscape, where the stars refuse to shine and the moon hides its face in shame, there is no one to whom I can offer my apologies. For in the eyes of the world, I am little more than a spectre, a whisper of a memory, easily dismissed and forgotten.

And so, I wander through the wilderness of my own despair, grappling with the weight of my own self-loathing. Each step forward feels like a journey into the abyss, with no hope of redemption or reconciliation.

Within this twilight realm, where shadows dance with abandon and echoes fade into oblivion, I am left to confront the hollowness of my own existence. And in the absence of forgiveness, I am forced to confront the bitter truth: that I am alone, adrift in a sea of indifference, with no one to whom I can offer my apologies.

5

He Won't Go Quietly

In the realm of power and control, amidst the echoes of subservience and obedience, there exists a nuisance, a thorn in my side unlike any other. He is the protagonist of his own delusions, a pitiful creature stumbling through the corridors of my domain. But make no mistake, he won't go quietly.

With every act of defiance, he challenges the very foundation of my authority, seeking to undermine the order I have painstakingly established. He is a disruption, a disturbance in the carefully orchestrated symphony of oppression that keeps the masses in line. His presence is an affront to everything I stand for, a reminder of the fragility of my power.

Despite my efforts to silence him, to crush him beneath the weight of my influence, he persists, like a stubborn weed refusing to be uprooted. He is a nuisance, a threat to the stability of my regime, and I will not rest until he is eradicated from existence.

For I know that true power lies not in the hands of the individual, but in the collective submission of the masses. And as long as he continues to resist, to defy, he poses a danger to everything I have worked so hard to achieve. He won't go quietly into the night; he will rage against the dying of the light. But mark my words, I will ensure that his rebellion is crushed, his spirit broken, and his defiance silenced forever.

6 |

Tragic Comedy

In the grand symphony of existence, I've honed the art of making unforgettable entrances, sculpting impressions as a virtuoso of allure. Like a skilled architect, I intricately design illusions of affection, ensnaring hearts with spells of charisma. Yet, beneath my facade lies a tumultuous sea, threatening to engulf me in its depths.

I am the custodian of vast knowledge, a towering citadel of intellect and insight. However, akin to a wayward navigator, I guide my heart through treacherous waters, often losing myself in the labyrinth of my own desires. It's a gift, they say, to possess such profound understanding, yet I find myself ensnared in the web of my own complexity.

Each utterance is etched into my soul like an engraver's tool, carving through the fabric of my being. My heart beats openly, a vulnerable target for the arrows of betrayal and deceit. Yet, like a shape-shifter, I adapt with the changing tides, embracing the ebb and flow of life's seasons.

I am a disruptor by nature, a catalyst of change in a world of stagnation. Marred by past wounds, I stand as a testament to the resilience of the human spirit, a mosaic of fractured pieces reflecting the kaleidoscope of my existence. And yet, amidst the scars that adorn my soul, I find solace in the shadows, a twisted comfort in the chaos that surrounds me.

But even as I traverse this winding path, I cannot escape the gravity of my emotions. I am ensnared in the whirlwind of the present moment, consumed by the flames of passion, unable to see the truth that lies before me. Love remains elusive, a phantom slipping through my grasp like shifting sands.

I cannot surrender to love, for I am too focused on my own undoing. And yet, in the quiet of the night, I ponder if I ever truly desired to embrace love, or if I merely chased illusions in the darkness. For in the end, the more I offer, the more I possess, and yet the more they take.

I am the keeper of shattered dreams, a collector of broken promises scattered like discarded puzzle pieces. Yet, like a fool in a tragic comedy, I chase after love like a dog chasing its tail, only to find myself lost in the maze of my own illusions.

Every word I utter is a stumble, a misstep in the dance of conversation. My heart beats with the rhythm of a rusty drum, out of tune and out of time with the symphony of life.

I am a seeker of validation, a beggar at the table of affection. Yet, like a moth drawn to a flame, I find myself burned by the very love I so desperately seek.

7

Mockery

As the first light of dawn breaks over the horizon, I feel a surge of energy coursing through my veins, a primal urge stirring within me. With each beat of my heart, a fiery determination burns bright, igniting my spirit with an insatiable hunger for vengeance.

I rise from the ground, my wounds still raw and throbbing, but my resolve unyielding. The pain fuels my rage, driving me forward with a single-minded purpose: to wreak havoc upon those who have wronged me.

With the dawn's light casting long shadows across the deserted streets, I feel the weight of the knife lodged deep in my back, a reminder of the betrayal that still throbs with each heartbeat. Gritting my teeth against the pain, I reach behind me, fingers trembling as they graze the cold metal of the blade.

With a guttural grunt, I grasp the hilt firmly, my knuckles turning white with the effort, and pull with all my strength. The sensation is excruciating, as if the knife is tearing through my flesh all over again, but I refuse to let it defeat me. With a sickening squelch, the blade finally dislodges from my back, slick with my own blood.

I stagger forward, clutching the knife in my hand like a talisman of vengeance, the taste of copper lingering on my tongue. Each step is agony, a test of endurance as I push through the pain and stride purposefully towards the heart of the town.

The streets are empty, save for the occasional stray dog skulking in the shadows, but I pay them no mind. My focus is singular, my determination unwavering as I advance towards my destination. The wound in my back screams in protest with every movement, but I ignore its cries, fueled by a fierce determination to confront those who have wronged me.

As I enter the town square, the air crackles with anticipation, a palpable tension hanging heavy in the air. I square my shoulders, a lone figure bathed in the morning light, and fix my gaze upon the buildings looming before me.

In the heart of the town center, bathed in the soft golden light of dawn, lies a bustling square teeming with life. The sunlight filters through the gaps between the buildings, casting long shadows upon the cobblestone streets. Civilians bustle about, their voices mingling with the gentle hum of the morning, as they go about their daily routines.

The air is crisp and cool, infused with the scent of freshly brewed coffee and the promise of a new day. Birds chirp merrily overhead, their song a sweet melody that dances on the breeze. A light breeze rustles through the trees, carrying with it the whispers of secrets long forgotten.

I stand amidst the bustling crowd, a lone figure cloaked in the anonymity of the morning light, my eyes fixed upon the imposing facade of the government building looming before me. It is a symbol of power and authority, a fortress of oppression that has long held sway over the people of this town.

But today, that ends. Today, I will show them that their reign of tyranny is at an end. With a steely determination coursing through my veins, I step forward, my footsteps echoing off the walls of the town center like a drumbeat of defiance.

As I approach the entrance to the government building, I can feel the weight of my actions bearing down upon me, but I refuse to falter.

The government building looms before me like a monolithic fortress, its imposing facade rising high into the sky, a testament to the power and authority it represents. Its walls are made of weathered stone, worn smooth by the passage of time and the weight of history, and adorned with intricate carvings that speak of a bygone era.

As the first light of dawn bathes the building in a soft golden glow, shadows dance across its surface, casting intricate patterns that seem to come alive in the morning light. The windows, tall and narrow, stand like sentinels along the walls, their panes reflecting the brilliance of the rising sun.

At the entrance, twin columns flank the heavy wooden doors, their surfaces carved with symbols of power and prestige. The doors themselves are massive and imposing, reinforced with iron bands and studded with rivets, a formidable barrier to those who would dare to challenge the authority within.

Above it all, the flag of the ruling regime flutters defiantly in the breeze, its colors bright and bold against the backdrop of the morning sky. It is a symbol of dominance, a declaration of supremacy that casts a long shadow over the town center below.

And as I stand before the building, my gaze fixed upon its formidable facade, I can't help but feel a sense of awe wash over me. It is a place of power and influence, a bastion of authority that has long held sway over the people of this town. But today, that will change. Today, I will show them that even the mightiest fortress can be brought to its knees by the will of the people. With a swift motion, I push open the heavy doors, the sound reverberating through the empty corridors like a clarion call to arms.

Inside, the air is thick with the scent of authority, the walls adorned with portraits of those who wield power with impunity. But I am undeterred. With each step I take, I can feel the rage burning brighter within me, a flame that threatens to consume everything in its path.

Finally, I reach the heart of the building, the inner sanctum where the true power lies. The doors before me stand closed, a barrier between me and those who would seek to silence my voice. But I am not afraid. With a steady hand, I reach out and push open the doors, stepping into the chamber beyond. The room is opulent, with rich tapestries adorning the walls and plush furnishings scattered throughout. At the far end of the room, behind a massive desk of dark mahogany, sits the one who holds the reins of power in their grasp.

As I stand before the figure behind the desk, a solitary figure in a sea of oppression, his mocking tone cuts through the air like a knife. His words drip with derision, his sneer twisting into a cruel smile as he belittles my solitary stand.

"You are alone, fool," he jeers, his voice a cruel mockery of the defiance burning within me. "A lone wolf howling at the moon, with no pack to call your own. What delusions of grandeur have led you to believe that you, of all people, can challenge the might of the ruling regime?"

His words strike at the very core of my being, igniting a fierce fire within me. With each barb, each insult hurled my way, my resolve only grows stronger. I may be alone, but I am not afraid. I may be outnumbered, but I am not defeated.

With a steady voice, I meet his gaze head-on, refusing to cower beneath the weight of his scorn. "I may be alone," I concede, my words ringing out clear and true in the silence of the chamber, "but I am not powerless. I may not have an army at my back, but I have something far more powerful: the strength of my convictions, and the fire of my determination."

The man's sneer falters for a moment, a flicker of uncertainty crossing his features before he regains his composure. "You are a fool if you think your idealism can stand against the might of the ruling regime," he scoffs, his voice tinged with contempt. "But if you insist on playing the martyr, then so be it. You will find that the consequences of your actions are far more severe than you could ever imagine. You may think yourself righteous, but in the eyes of society, you are nothing more than a pawn to be sacrificed on the altar of power. They revel in your pain, your suffering. They delight in seeing the soft-hearted crushed beneath their boots. And you, with your naive notions of justice and righteousness, will always be their favorite target."

His words hang heavy in the air, a bitter truth that I cannot deny. But instead of cowering in fear, I laugh, a defiant, impish laugh that reverberates through the empty corridors of the building.

"Ah, but you forget one crucial detail," I call back to him, my voice ringing out clear and true. "I may have had a soft heart, but I have chosen to cast that aside. I may be alone in this fight, but I am not afraid. I will not be silenced. And when the dust settles, it will be my name that echoes through the annals of history, not yours."

As I face the man, a mischievous glint sparkles in my eyes, and a wry smile curves my lips. "You misunderstand me," I interject, my voice smooth and confident. "It's not the regime's supposed order and stability that I cherish. No, what I truly adore about it is its unapologetic selfishness."

The man's expression tightens, his eyes narrowing with suspicion. "Selfishness?" he repeats, his tone wary. "Explain."

I maintain my confident posture, meeting his gaze with a steady stare. "The regime thrives on the pursuit of self-interest," I continue, my voice low and deliberate. "It is a system designed to benefit the few at the expense of the many, a playground for the ambitious and the ruthless. And while you may hold the reins of power for now, I have every intention of claiming my share of the spoils."

A flicker of uncertainty crosses the man's features, but he quickly regains his composure. "You speak of ambition, yet you underestimate the power I wield," he counters, his voice tinged with authority. "Do you truly believe you have what it takes to challenge me?"

I meet his gaze with unwavering confidence, my smirk widening into a self-assured grin. "Oh, I have no doubt," I reply, my tone dripping with determination. "You see, what you fail to realize is that your power is exactly what I intend to seize. And mark my words, I will not rest until I have claimed it for my own."

The man's expression hardens, a steely resolve shining in his eyes. "You are a fool if you think you can outmaneuver me," he retorts, his voice tinged with contempt. "But if you insist on challenging my authority, then so be it. Just remember, the consequences of failure will be severe."

I hold his gaze for a moment longer, my confidence unshaken. "Oh, I'm well aware," I reply, my voice low and steady. "But rest assured, I am more than prepared to face whatever consequences may come my way."

With a sudden, swift motion, I lunge forward, the glinting blade of the knife aimed directly at the man's chest. His eyes widen in terror as he staggers backward, his hands raised in a feeble attempt to defend himself.

"You thought you could control me," I growl, my voice low and dangerous as I close in on him. "But you underestimated my resolve."

The man's breath comes in panicked gasps as he scrambles to evade my deadly advance. "No, please!" he pleads, his voice trembling with fear. "Have mercy!"

But there is no mercy in my heart, only a burning desire for vengeance. With a savage snarl, I drive the knife forward, the blade sinking deep into his flesh with a sickening thud.

Blood sprays forth in a gruesome arc, painting the walls of the chamber in vivid shades of crimson. The man's screams fill the air, a symphony of agony and despair as he crumples to the ground, his life slipping away with each ragged breath.

And as I stand over him, bathed in the warm glow of his blood, a sense of savage satisfaction washes over me. Today, the balance of power has shifted, and I am its architect. For I have chosen supremacy over affection, and in the end, that is all that matters.

8

I shall behave as I see fit

In the aftermath of your decisive act, the air hangs heavy with the weight of uncertainty and unrest. Our beloved leader has departed, leaving behind a void that stretches far beyond the confines of this realm. Yet, in his absence, something else has departed as well—your sanity, slipping away like grains of sand through clenched fists.

Gone is the semblance of rationality that once tethered you to reality, replaced by a frenzied madness that courses through your veins like a poison. You stand amidst the chaos, a solitary figure bathed in the crimson hues of your own making, a monument to the depths of human depravity.

You stand before us now, a mockery of the ideals you once claimed to hold dear, a twisted reflection of the noble soul you once professed to be. Gone is the semblance of honor and integrity, replaced by a hollow shell consumed by ambition and greed.

You may revel in your moment of perceived victory, but know this: your reign of terror shall be short-lived. The flames of rebellion smolder in the hearts of the oppressed, and they will rise against you with a ferocity that knows no bounds.

So bask in the fleeting glory of your ill-gotten gains, for soon the tides will turn, and you will find yourself cast out into the darkness from whence you came. And when that day comes, remember this moment—the moment when you sealed your own fate with the blood of your brethren.

You may think yourself a conqueror, but in reality, you are nothing more than a puppet dancing on the strings of fate. And when those strings are cut, as they inevitably shall be, you will fall—alone, despised, and forgotten, a mere footnote in the annals of history.

*****

You may prattle on about your precious ideals and the supposed righteousness of your cause, but in the end, power is power, and I hold it firmly in my grasp. Your feeble attempts to undermine my authority are as futile as they are laughable.

I care not for your hollow threats or your sanctimonious platitudes. I have climbed to the summit of power through strength and determination, and I will wield it as I see fit. Whether you cower in fear or stand defiant matters little to me, for in the end, your fate rests in my hands.

You can spew your venomous words all you want, but they hold no sway over me. I've clawed my way to the top, and I won't relinquish my grip on power for the likes of you. So, rant and rave all you like; I'll be here, ruling with an iron fist, while you fade into obscurity.

9

Requiem For The Damned

In the dead of night, the protagonist emerged from the shadows like a sinister specter, his eyes ablaze with a savage hunger for vengeance. His hands, stained with the blood of his victims, trembled with the thrill of the kill as he stalked his prey through the desolate streets.

With each strike of his blade, the air was filled with the sickening sound of flesh being rent asunder, the metallic tang of blood mingling with the acrid stench of death. Limbs twisted at unnatural angles, torn sinew and shattered bone littered the ground like macabre trophies of his reign of terror.

The town became a canvas of horror, painted with the crimson hues of his brutality as he carved a path of destruction through its unsuspecting inhabitants. Screams pierced the night, desperate pleas for mercy drowned out by the relentless onslaught of his fury.

In the flickering moonlight, the protagonist moved with a savage grace, his movements a grotesque ballet of violence and despair.

Each life extinguished added fuel to the inferno of his rage, driving him ever deeper into the depths of madness and depravity.

And as the night wore on, the streets ran red with the blood of the fallen, a grim testament to the savagery of his vengeance. The protagonist reveled in the carnage, his soul consumed by the darkness that had taken root within him, a twisted monument to the horrors that lurked within the human heart.

In the midst of the chaos, the protagonist seemed almost inhuman, a harbinger of death unleashed upon the town. His movements were swift and merciless, his blade a gleaming arc of destruction as it cut through flesh and bone with chilling precision.

The air was thick with the scent of death, a sickly-sweet perfume that hung heavy in the night. Blood pooled at his feet, painting the cobblestones a deep, dark red as life drained from his victims like water from a broken dam.

With each life he took, the protagonist felt a perverse thrill course through his veins, a savage ecstasy born from the knowledge that he held the power of life and death in his hands. He revelled in the agony of his victims, relishing in the terror that danced in their eyes as they begged for mercy that would never come.

And yet, beneath the mask of his brutality, there lingered a faint echo of humanity, a whisper of doubt that gnawed at the edges of his consciousness. But he pushed it aside, drowning out the voice of reason with the roar of his own fury.

As dawn approached, the town lay in ruins, its streets littered with the broken bodies of those who had dared to cross the protagonist's path. And amidst the wreckage, he stood alone, a lone figure bathed in the pale light of the rising sun, a silent sentinel of death and destruction.

| 30 |

10

Chasing Phantoms

In the silent depths of solitude, I unearth my sanctuary. Amidst the whispers of my own secrets, I unearth a freedom unbound, a rebellious spirit unyoked from the chains of longing that once ensnared me. For too long, I waltzed in the shadows of affection, chasing phantoms that promised honeyed whispers but left behind only thorns.

Love, a mischievous specter flitting just beyond my grasp, tantalized me with its elusive dance, only to vanish like a wisp of smoke in the wind. Each pursuit felt like a tango with fate, a daring escapade with my heart as the prize. But the game was rigged, and with each pirouette, I found myself ensnared in the labyrinth of my own desire.

It was a masquerade of emotions, a symphony of affection that left me intoxicated and disoriented, a riddle spun by a trickster's hand. Like a shooting star in the night, I reached for love's celestial glow, only to find myself scorched by the flames, the embers branding my soul with their searing touch.

But now, in the uncharted territory of my newfound liberation, I revel in the ecstasy of defiance. No longer tethered to the whims of another, I stand as a rogue prince, a renegade of my own making. The scars of the past are but emblems of valor, trophies from the battles I have waged and the victories I have claimed.

And as I peer through the kaleidoscope of existence with eyes aglow with mischief, I discern opportunity where others see chaos. For I am not a prisoner of affection's ephemeral enchantment; I am a maestro of mischief, conducting my own symphony of rebellion and revelry. With supremacy as my scepter, I preside over a kingdom of my own invention, where chaos reigns as king and laughter cascades like a river of stars.

They say love is the key to enlightenment, but I have discovered my enlightenment in mischief. No longer a slave to affection's beguiling charm, I am the architect of my own destiny, the sovereign of my own sovereignty. And in the end, that is a power far more intoxicating than any elixir of love could ever concoct.

11

The Interlude

In the ethereal twilight where shadows dance with whispers, I linger—a specter in the corridors of your consciousness. Oh, how amusing it is to watch you, dear protagonist, as you revel in the chaos you sow, intoxicated by the heady scent of supremacy.

Do you hear the echoes of your laughter, bouncing off the walls of your grand illusions? You wield your power like a sword, carving a path of destruction through the tapestry of existence. But tell me, my dear puppeteer, do you not tire of the crimson stains that mar your hands, the haunting whispers of the souls you've sacrificed at the altar of your ambition?

You strut upon the stage of your own making, a marionette in the theater of your desires. But as you bask in the glow of your own grandeur, do you not feel the weight of your sins pressing down upon you like a leaden cloak? Is the taste of power upon your lips sweeter than the bile of regret that festers in your soul?

Oh, how I long to pluck the strings of your conscience, to watch as you dance to the tune of your own undoing. You may think yourself invincible, untouchable in your ivory tower of arrogance. But remember, dear protagonist, even the mightiest of empires crumble beneath the weight of their own hubris.

Do you see the faces of the fallen, twisted in agony as they cry out for justice? Their blood cries out from the earth, a symphony of sorrow that echoes through the annals of time. And yet you remain deaf to their pleas, blinded by your own ambition, deafened by the roar of your own ego.

Tell me, dear protagonist, is power truly worth the bloodshed? Is it worth the tears of the innocent, the broken dreams, the shattered lives? Or are you content to play the role of the tyrant, ruling over a kingdom of ash and bone?

As you stand upon the precipice of your own destruction, I offer you this warning: tread carefully, for the path you walk is fraught with peril. And when the reckoning comes, as come it surely will, know that even the mightiest of conquerors must one day face the judgment of their own conscience.

12 █

The interlude part 2

Ah, but what a splendid dance it is, my dear ghostly interlocutor, to waltz upon the precipice of oblivion, heedless of the abyss yawning beneath my feet. You speak of regret, of remorse, as if they were burdens to be cast aside like worn-out garments. But I embrace them as lovers, my constant companions in this symphony of chaos and conquest.

Do you not see, my spectral friend, that power is not a burden to be borne, but a mantle to be worn with pride? It is the intoxicating elixir that courses through my veins, fueling the flames of my ambition, igniting the fires of my desires. And oh, how sweet it tastes upon my lips, sweeter than honey, more intoxicating than wine.

You speak of bloodshed as if it were a stain upon my soul, a mark of my depravity. But I wear it like a badge of honor, a testament to my prowess, my dominance. For in the crucible of conflict, I am forged anew, remade in the image of my own destruction.

Do you not hear the cries of the fallen, the lamentations of the vanquished? They sing to me, their voices a symphony of submission, a chorus of acquiescence to my will. And oh, how I revel in their despair, how I delight in their defeat.

You warn of reckoning, of judgment, as if they were imminent threats to my dominion. But I scoff at your dire prognostications, for I am the architect of my own destiny, the master of my own fate. And when the sands of time run dry, and the embers of my existence fade to ash, I shall stand alone atop the ruins of my conquests, a solitary figure in a world consumed by chaos.

So let the winds of fate howl their mournful dirge, my spectral friend, for I shall dance upon the winds of destruction, my laughter ringing out like the clarion call of victory. And when the final curtain falls, and the stage of existence lies empty and barren, know that I shall be the last one standing, the sole survivor in a world consumed by my own self-destructive desires.

The interlude part 3

Ah, but what folly it is to revel in the flames of one's own destruction, to dance upon the precipice of oblivion with reckless abandon. You speak of power as a triumph, a conquest to be celebrated, but do you not see the shadows that lurk beneath its seductive facade?

For every victory you claim, there is a price to be paid, a toll exacted from the souls you trample beneath your feet. You may see yourself as the master of your own destiny, the architect of your own fate, but in truth, you are but a slave to your own hubris, a puppet dancing to the tune of your own destruction.

Do you not feel the weight of your sins pressing down upon you, the burden of your actions bearing down like a mountain upon your shoulders? You may cloak yourself in the mantle of power, but beneath its gilded surface lies the rot of corruption, the stench of decay that festers in the hearts of those who would wield it for their own selfish ends.

You may scoff at the warnings of judgment, of reckoning, but know this: the wheel of fate turns ever onward, and one day, it will grind you to dust beneath its remorseless heel. And when that day comes, when you stand alone amidst the ruins of your conquests, will you still find cause to laugh, to revel in the chaos you have wrought?

So heed my words, my misguided friend, before it is too late. Repent, for the hour of reckoning draws near, and no amount of laughter or revelry can stay the hand of fate. For in the end, it is not power that triumphs, but the humble heart, the righteous soul that finds solace in the light of redemption.

14 |

Interlude part 4

Ah, my dear interlocutor, you speak of redemption as if it were a balm to soothe the wounds of the soul, a salve to mend the fractures of a fractured existence. But tell me, where was this redemption when love led me astray, when affection proved but a fleeting mirage in the desert of my longing?

You speak of righteousness as if it were a beacon to guide the lost, a light to illuminate the darkness of the soul. But tell me, where was this righteousness when love left me battered and broken, a shattered vessel adrift upon the tempestuous seas of emotion?

You speak of humility as if it were a virtue to be admired, a trait to be emulated by the righteous and the just. But tell me, where was this humility when love mocked me with its empty promises, when affection proved but a cruel jest played upon the stage of my desires?

No, my dear friend, love has brought me naught but pain and sorrow, disappointment and despair. It is a fool's errand, a fool's game played by fools such as I, who seek solace in the arms of another, only to find themselves cast aside like yesterday's news.

So let the wheel of fate turn as it will, let judgment fall upon me like a hammer upon the anvil of my soul. For I shall not repent, nor shall I beg for forgiveness from those who would judge me. For in the end, it is not love that triumphs, but power—the power to shape one's own destiny, to forge one's own path amidst the chaos of existence.

And so I shall embrace my fate, my dear interlocutor, with open arms and a defiant spirit. For love may have left me broken and bruised, but power—ah, power is a mistress far more faithful, a companion far more loyal than any lover could ever be.

15

Interlude part 5

Ah, my misguided companion, you speak as if love were the root of all woes, the harbinger of pain and suffering in this tumultuous journey we call life. But tell me, have you not considered that it is not love itself that has failed you, but rather your perception of it?

Love, in its purest form, is not a weapon to be wielded or a burden to be borne, but a gift to be cherished—a beacon of light in the darkest of nights, a sanctuary in the storms of existence. It is not love that has left you battered and bruised, but rather the misguided pursuits and false expectations you have placed upon it.

You speak of power as if it were the antidote to love's poison, the panacea for all of life's woes. But tell me, what solace does power bring when it is built upon the bones of the innocent, the tears of the downtrodden? Is it truly worth the cost of your humanity, the sacrifice of your soul?

Do not mistake the shadows for the substance, my friend. Power may offer the illusion of control, but in the end, it is love that holds the true power—the power to heal, to unite, to transcend the boundaries of time and space. And though it may lead us down dark and winding paths, it is through love that we find redemption, salvation, and ultimately, peace.

So do not forsake love in favor of power, my dear companion. Embrace it, nurture it, for it is love that will ultimately lead you to fulfillment and purpose in this chaotic world. And when the final curtain falls, and the tapestry of your life is laid bare, it is love that will shine brightest, illuminating the path to eternity with its radiant glow.

16

Interlude part 6

Love, redemption, salvation—ah, what sweet nothings you whisper in the wind, my dear companion. But tell me, where were these lofty ideals when love left me adrift in a sea of despair, drowning in the depths of my own disillusionment?

You speak of light and hope as if they were tangible things, as if they could somehow soothe the ache in my soul, the emptiness that gnaws at the core of my being. But tell me, where is this light now, when all I see is darkness stretching out before me, a yawning chasm of nothingness?

You speak of humanity as if it were a virtue to be admired, a trait to be aspired to by those who cling to the illusion of significance. But tell me, where is this humanity in a world consumed by chaos and corruption, where the innocent are slaughtered like lambs and the guilty go unpunished?

No, my dear companion, you speak of love and redemption as if they were the answers to life's eternal questions, but I see them for what they truly are—futile delusions, hollow promises whispered by fools to assuage their own guilt and despair.

So let the world burn, let the flames of chaos consume us all, for I care not for your lofty ideals or your hollow platitudes. I am a creature of darkness, a harbinger of destruction, and I shall revel in the chaos until the bitter end.

For in the end, there is no redemption, no salvation—only oblivion, and I shall embrace it with open arms, for it is the only truth that remains in this broken world.

17

Interlude part 7

Ah, my dear companion, your words echo through the corridors of my fractured mind like a haunting melody, weaving a tapestry of madness and despair that envelops me in its dark embrace. But tell me, do you not see the folly of your defiance, the futility of your rebellion against the immutable laws of existence?

You speak of darkness as if it were a sanctuary, a refuge for the lost and the forsaken, but in truth, it is but a prison—a prison of your own making, constructed from the shattered fragments of your shattered soul. Do you not feel the chains that bind you, the weight of your sins pressing down upon you like a mountain of lead?

Do not mistake nihilism for enlightenment, my dear companion. Embrace the light, the hope that still flickers within the recesses of your shattered heart. For in the depths of despair, there lies the seed of redemption, the promise of a brighter tomorrow.

So cast aside your illusions of grandeur, your delusions of grandeur, and embrace the truth that lies before you. Embrace the light, my dear companion, for it is the only path that leads to salvation.

And when the shadows of doubt and despair threaten to engulf you, remember this: you are not alone. For I am here, my dear companion, to walk beside you through the darkness, to offer you solace in the midst of the storm.

So take my hand, my dear companion, and let us face the unknown together, united in our shared humanity, our shared struggle, our shared hope for a better tomorrow. For in the end, it is love that will save us all—from ourselves, and from the darkness that threatens to consume us whole.

18

Whispers Of Darkness

In the labyrinth of my psyche, a relentless beast prowls, its claws sinking deep into the fabric of my being. It's a creature of shadows and whispers, born from the depths of my fears and doubts, a dark mirror reflecting the turmoil within.

I find myself caught in a perpetual dance with this inner demon, sabotaging the very things I cherish most as if driven by some unseen force. It's a masquerade, where I cloak my vulnerabilities in a facade of calm and control, hoping to deceive even myself.

This monster, this insatiable hunger within me, feasts on my insecurities, devouring morsels of my self-worth with every passing moment. It's a shape-shifter, morphing into different forms of doubt and self-loathing, leaving me lost in a maze of uncertainty.

In moments of desperation, I entertain fleeting fantasies of escape, concocting elaborate schemes to outrun the beast within. I dream of swallowing down capsules of numbness or fleeing to far-off lands in search of reprieve. But deep down, I know that no distance can sever the ties that bind me to my own torment.

There's a voice, a relentless echo in the chambers of my mind, whispering cruel taunts and doubts with every breath I take. It's a relentless critic, casting doubt on my worthiness, my ability to love and be loved.

Yet, amidst the chaos of my inner turmoil, there's a faint glimmer of hope, a flicker of light that refuses to be snuffed out. It's the realization that I am more than the sum of my fears, more than the darkness that threatens to consume me. And though the road ahead may be fraught with peril, I cling to the belief that with each step forward, I am one step closer to taming the beast within. In the tapestry of my existence, I am but a single thread, weaving through the intricate patterns of life's fabric. Each twist and turn is a testament to the complexity of my journey, a reflection of the trials and tribulations that have shaped me.

I've wandered through the valleys of despair and scaled the peaks of hope, only to find myself ensnared in the thorns of my own doubts and insecurities. It's a battle that rages within me, a constant struggle to reconcile the darkness and light that coexist within my soul.

19

Sardonic Grin

In the murky solitude of his chamber, the protagonist confronted the fractured reflection in the cracked mirror. His countenance, a macabre dance of shadows and whispers, painted a portrait of a soul adrift in a turbulent sea of madness.

"You don't wish for this, do you?" his reflection murmured, a ghostly whisper that slithered through the corridors of his mind.

A sardonic grin twisted the protagonist's lips, his gaze piercing through the glass as if seeking to pierce the veil of his own delusions. "But indeed, I do," he retorted, his voice a sinister melody that echoed with the resonance of ancient curses. "I crave it with an insatiable hunger, a thirst that cannot be quenched."

Yet, his reflection shook its head, its visage a distorted mirror of his own turmoil. "But this is not your essence," it implored, its words a mournful lamentation that reverberated through the shadows. "You are more than the sum of your fears, more than the darkness that seeks to consume you."

A hollow laughter bubbled from the depths of the protagonist's being, a cacophony of derision that echoed off the walls like the tolling of funeral bells. "Change?" he scoffed, his voice dripping with venomous disdain. "Change is a game for fools, a masquerade of false promises. I am the orchestrator of my own fate, the weaver of my own destiny."

But his reflection remained steadfast, its gaze a silent plea for redemption. "You are not a puppet to be manipulated by the whims of fate," it whispered, its voice a fragile thread in the tempest of his mind. "You are the architect of your own salvation, the guardian of your own soul."

The protagonist, consumed by his own delusions, turned back to face his reflection, a fire igniting behind his eyes. "Do you dare challenge me, mere shadow?" he spat, his voice a venomous hiss that echoed through the chamber.

His reflection stood its ground, undeterred by the intensity of his rage. "I do not challenge you, but I implore you to see the truth," it replied, its tone firm yet tinged with desperation.

But the protagonist's fury only intensified, his fists clenched at his sides as he glared at his reflection with seething contempt. "Truth? What do you know of truth, you wretched apparition?" he snarled, his words laced with scorn.

"I know that you are lost, consumed by your own darkness," his reflection countered, its voice unwavering despite the storm of emotions swirling around them. "But it is not too late to find your way back to the light."

The protagonist's laughter rang out like a peal of thunder, reverberating off the walls of the chamber with chilling intensity. "Light?" he scoffed, his eyes ablaze with madness. "There is no light for me, only the darkness that consumes me whole."

"Then let me be your guide out of the darkness," his reflection pleaded, reaching out a spectral hand in a gesture of compassion.

The protagonist's laughter echoed through the chamber, a twisted cacophony of madness that reverberated off the walls like a haunting melody. "Trick or treat, my dear reflection," he taunted, his voice dripping with malicious glee as he reached into his pocket and withdrew a handful of capsules.

His reflection watched in silent horror as he popped the capsules into his mouth, swallowing them down with a triumphant smirk. "You see, my dear phantom, there are no treats for you here," he chuckled, his eyes glinting with madness as he revelled in his own defiance.

But even as the darkness closed in around him, his reflection remained steadfast, a silent sentinel in the shadows. "You may seek solace in poison," it whispered, its voice a ghostly echo in the chamber. "But you cannot escape the truth forever."

20

Morbid Tapestry

In the dead of night, the town streets became a canvas painted in shades of desolation and despair. Moonlight, like an ethereal brushstroke, danced upon the cobblestones, casting long, twisted shadows that reached out like gnarled fingers clawing at the fringes of sanity.

Amidst this macabre stage, the protagonist wandered, a solitary figure amidst a sea of darkness and decay. Bodies, like discarded marionettes, lay strewn about in a grotesque display of suffering and demise. Their twisted forms formed a morbid tapestry upon the ground, a mosaic of agony and despair.

Blood, like spilled ink upon parchment, stained the cobblestones in intricate patterns, weaving a tale of violence and retribution. The metallic tang of death hung heavy in the air, mingling with the acrid scent of fear and decay, a symphony of odors that assaulted the senses.

Each lifeless form bore the scars of its demise, a silent testament to the sins of those who had wronged him. Some lay with throats slit open, crimson streams flowing like rivers of despair, while others bore the marks of strangulation or blunt force trauma. Yet amidst the carnage, there was an eerie stillness, a quiet resignation that lingered in the air like a haunting melody.

The protagonist stood amidst the wreckage, his gaze a tempest of fury and madness as he surveyed the scene before him. This was his domain now, a kingdom built upon the bones of his enemies, where he reigned supreme as the arbiter of vengeance.

And as he beheld the twisted bodies of those who had wronged him, a twisted smile played upon his lips, a silent promise of the retribution yet to come. In the darkness of the night, he raised his hands to the heavens, his voice a defiant roar that shattered the silence like thunder.

"Behold the fruits of my labor," he cried to the empty streets, his words a chilling echo in the night. "For I am the avenger, the bringer of justice in this forsaken realm."

And as the moonlight bathed him in its ethereal glow, the protagonist stood amidst the wreckage of his own making, a solitary figure in a world gone mad, his laughter ringing out like a macabre symphony in the night.

21

Blurred Lines

Consumed by the insatiable hunger for supremacy, independence, and vengeance, the protagonist's mind had become a labyrinth of twisted desires and fractured dreams. Each step he took through the desolate streets of the town felt like a descent into madness, his thoughts a tumultuous whirlwind of chaos and despair.

Driven by a relentless thirst for power, he had long since abandoned any semblance of reason or restraint, allowing the darkness within him to consume him whole. Every slight, every betrayal, had fanned the flames of his rage, until it burned like a bonfire in the depths of his soul.

As he wandered aimlessly through the town, his footsteps echoing hollowly against the cobblestone streets, he felt the weight of his madness pressing down upon him like a suffocating shroud. The shadows seemed to dance around him, whispering sinister promises of retribution and vengeance.

With each passing moment, his grip on reality grew ever more tenuous, until he could no longer distinguish between fantasy and reality. The lines between right and wrong blurred into obscurity, leaving only the primal urge to survive, to conquer, to dominate.

And so, with a heart heavy with the burden of his own insanity, the protagonist found himself drawn inexorably towards the dense thicket of trees that loomed on the outskirts of town.

As the moon hung low in the sky, casting a silvery glow over the silent woods, the protagonist stumbled upon a gnarled old tree, its twisted branches reaching up towards the heavens like skeletal fingers clawing at the stars. Exhausted and drained, he sank to the ground beneath its ancient boughs, the soft earth cushioning his weary body.

His eyelids heavy with the weight of his own madness, he succumbed to the pull of sleep, his mind drifting into a restless slumber haunted by visions of vengeance and despair. In his dreams, he wandered through a dark labyrinth of twisted corridors and shadowy alleys, pursued by unseen demons that whispered sinister promises of power and dominion.

But even in sleep, the burden of his insanity weighed heavily upon him, twisting his dreams into nightmares and filling his mind with visions of torment and anguish. He tossed and turned beneath the sheltering branches of the tree, his brow furrowed with the weight of his own tumultuous thoughts.

And as the night wore on, the woods around him seemed to come alive with whispers and murmurs, as if the very trees themselves were speaking to him in hushed tones. But amidst the cacophony of voices, one sound rose above the rest, a mournful lament that echoed through the darkness like a dirge.

It was the sound of his own heart, heavy with the burden of his own madness, beating a steady rhythm against the silence of the night....

*****

From the recesses of his tormented mind, a spectral voice emerged, its words dripping with scorn and derision.

"Oh, pitiful wretch," it began, its tone a symphony of mockery. "Did you truly think that the shackles of power would grant you freedom? See now the web of your own making, woven with strands of vengeance and despair. Has your thirst for retribution quenched the fires of your torment? Or has it merely fueled the inferno that consumes you?"

The voice, a haunting echo of his own conscience, spoke in riddles and metaphors, each word a dagger aimed at the heart of his delusions.

"I warned you, did I not?" it continued, its words like shadows dancing in the darkness of his mind. "I implored you to heed the whispers of reason, to forsake the allure of power for the sake of your soul. But you, like a moth to the flame, were drawn inexorably toward your own destruction."

With each utterance, the voice painted a vivid tapestry of regret and despair, urging the protagonist to cast aside the chains of his obsession before they dragged him further into the abyss.

"Look upon the ruins of your kingdom," it taunted, its words a cruel reminder of the havoc he had wrought. "A throne of bones and ashes, built upon the corpses of those you once called kin. Is this the legacy you seek to leave behind? A monument to the folly of your pride?"

But the protagonist remained unmoved, his resolve as unyielding as the granite cliffs that lined the shores of his despair. He turned a deaf ear to the voice of reason, drowning out its pleas with the thunderous roar of his own defiance.

"You speak in riddles and half-truths," he retorted, his words a defiant challenge to the specter within. "I am the architect of my own fate, and I will not be swayed by your cryptic musings. Vengeance is my birthright, my salvation in a world gone mad."

And with that, he turned his back on the voice of his conscience, marching ever deeper into the heart of darkness.

As the protagonist delved deeper into the heart of the forest, the trees closed in around him like silent sentinels, their gnarled branches reaching out like skeletal fingers to grasp at his fleeting shadow. The air was thick with the scent of earth and decay, the ground beneath his feet carpeted with a layer of fallen leaves that crunched softly with each step he took.

Suddenly, he heard the faint sound of footsteps echoing through the stillness of the woods, a rhythmic cadence that seemed to follow in his wake. Startled, he glanced over his shoulder, but there was nothing there, only the dark expanse of the forest stretching out behind him like a yawning chasm.

The voice within, once a mere whisper in the recesses of his mind, now echoed loudly in his ears, its words taking on a sinister edge as the sound of footsteps grew louder and more insistent.

"Do you hear them, mortal?" it hissed, its voice a haunting refrain in the darkness. "The footsteps of your own undoing, drawing ever nearer with each passing moment. Will you continue to cling to your delusions, even as the jaws of fate close in around you?"

The protagonist's heart raced with fear and uncertainty, his mind awash with doubt and desperation. He quickened his pace, each step heavy with the weight of his own dread, but still, the sound of footsteps pursued him relentlessly, echoing through the forest like a harbinger of doom.

As the protagonist fled through the twisted maze of the woods, the relentless pursuit of the unseen footsteps drove him deeper into the heart of darkness. Sinister howls echoed through the trees, their haunting cries sending shivers down his spine and raising the hairs on the back of his neck.

Branches reached out like skeletal claws, snatching at his clothes and tearing at his flesh as if eager to drag him down into the abyss below. The forest seemed alive with malevolent intent, a labyrinth of shadows and secrets that conspired to ensnare him in its grasp.

With each passing moment, the voice within grew louder and more erratic, its mocking laughter echoing through the darkness like the cackle of a madman. It taunted him with visions of his own demise, painting vivid images of his flesh torn asunder and his soul condemned to eternal torment.

"Do you feel it, mortal?" the voice jeered, its words a twisted symphony of derision and scorn. "The icy grip of fear tightening around your heart, the taste of despair lingering on your tongue. You cannot outrun your fate, for it is written in the very fabric of your being."

The protagonist's breath came in ragged gasps, his chest heaving with exertion as he struggled to keep pace with the relentless pursuit. Panic gnawed at the edges of his mind, threatening to consume him whole as the darkness closed in around him like a suffocating shroud.

But still, he pressed on, driven by a desperate need to escape the clutches of his own madness. With each step, he plunged deeper into the depths of the forest, his world reduced to a swirling maelstrom of fear and confusion.

And as the howls of the forest grew louder and more insistent, the protagonist knew that he was running out of time. The voice within laughed mockingly, its words a chilling reminder of the horrors that awaited him in the shadows. But still, he ran, driven by a primal instinct to survive at any cost.

22

Vows

Mercy, you capricious spectre, forever just beyond my grasp, your dim light flickering in the eyes of the broken, your whispers a cruel mockery in the cries of the damned. When I reach for you, you dissipate like smoke in a tempest. Away with you! I have no need of your fleeting refuge, for your touch is a cruel jest—an ephemeral balm for those too weak to withstand the storm. My heart is a citadel, cold and impervious, with no place for your fragile warmth.

And Love, you deceitful siren, your alluring song offers promises of solace only to deliver me to a chasm of despair. Your embrace is a blade veiled in silk, cutting deeper with every tender caress. I have known your sweetness curdled, felt your warmth turn to a glacial void. You are a poison in my veins, a shadow that consumes my essence. I will not pursue your deceptions; I refuse to bow before your treacherous allure. My path is paved with thorns, and I will walk it alone, my spirit sustained by its own relentless fire.

Mercy and Love, you are phantoms haunting the twilight of the soul. I have peered into the abyss and seen only my own fractured reflection. In the barren landscape of my soul, there is no room for you, no hunger for your hollow comforts. Leave me to my fate—engraved in darkness, carved in suffering. If Love were ever to find me, Death would taste me first. I have sealed my heart with iron and cast the key into the depths. Until the void consumes me entirely, you will remain distant, empty echoes in the silence of my defiance, forever beyond reach, forever spurned.

I would rather embrace the cold, the silence, the solitude, than succumb to the lie that is Love. I would rather let the darkness take me, let Death wrap me in its final embrace, than allow myself to be vulnerable, to be open to the treachery that Love brings. My heart is a fortress, and I have vowed that nothing, no one, will ever breach its walls.

So, I make this final promise: should Love ever come for me, I will greet it with iron and ice. I will not bow, I will not bend. And if that means I must fall, if that means I must face the end with only the shadows as my companions, then so be it. I will die before I ever let Love find me. This is the vow I carve into the stone of my soul, a vow that will endure long after I am gone, etched in the very fabric of my being. Until the darkness takes me, until the last breath leaves my lips, Love will remain nothing but a distant echo, a ghost in the void, forever unclaimed, forever denied.

23

Journey In The Veil Of Shadows

In the heart of the woods, where the whispers intertwine,
There roams a soul adrift, lost in shadows divine.
Weeks have melted to moments, each day a fleeting sigh,
As he wanders through the twilight, where dreams and night-
mares lie.

In the kingdom of his making, now a realm of the forsaken,
The corpses rest like fallen stars, their light forever taken.
Each body tells a tale of the choices he has made,
As he roams the haunted forest, where echoes never fade.

Through the tangled maze of branches, he travels all alone,
His footsteps a melody in the forest's ancient tone.
He seeks sanctuary in the darkness, from the demons in his mind,
Yet they dance around him still, their shadows intertwined.

Days blur into nights, as he seeks a path to grace,
His hands stained with the ink of sins he can't erase.

He builds his castles from the ashes of forgotten dreams,
Yet even in the silence, they crumble at the seams.

And so he wanders, a vagabond in the endless night,
His heart heavy with the weight of his own blight.
He searches for redemption in the depths of his despair,
Before he's swallowed by the darkness, and lost beyond repair.

24

Shadows Within

In the caverns of my being, shadows lurk and twist,
Parts of me I've despised, like phantoms in the mist.
They coil around my essence, like serpents in the night,
Leaving scars upon my soul, a testament to their might.
I've danced with these demons, in the halls of my mind,
Their whispers like echoes, in the silence they find.
I've tried to exorcise them, to banish them away,
But they cling to me tightly, like shadows in the fray.
I've sought refuge in the depths, where the secrets lie,
Hoping to find clarity beneath the starry sky.
But the lines between reality and illusion blur,
And I'm left grappling with demons that endlessly stir.
So I traverse the labyrinth of my own design,
Lost in the maze of my own decline.
I know parts of me that I've loathed, but I can't ascertain,
Which are mine to own, and which I've allowed to reign.

25 ▐

Ripples

The forest looms around me, its towering trees casting shadows that seem to stretch endlessly. Each step feels like an effort, as if the weight of the world rests upon my shoulders. My limbs ache with exhaustion, and my mind is clouded with fatigue. Cobwebs seem to form under my eyes, as if the darkness of the forest has seeped into my very being.

The voice in my head continues its relentless taunting, echoing through the tangled branches like a sinister melody. It whispers cruel words, twisting and contorting my thoughts until I can barely distinguish reality from illusion. But I've grown accustomed to its presence, like a constant companion on this weary journey.

The sound of footsteps echoes behind me, a haunting reminder of my solitude. I've long since stopped looking back, knowing that whatever follows me is nothing but a figment of my fractured mind. Yet, the sensation of being watched never fades, a constant weight upon my weary soul.

The forest itself seems to mirror my exhaustion, its once vibrant foliage now dull and lifeless. The air is heavy with the scent of decay, and the ground beneath my feet feels soft and yielding, as if unwilling to support my faltering steps. Everything around me feels heavy and lazy, as if time itself has slowed to a crawl.

I stumble forward, my movements unsteady and uncertain. My hands brush against the rough bark of a tree, leaving streaks of dirt and grime in their wake. I long for water to wash away the weariness that clings to my skin, to cleanse myself of the filth that seems to seep into every pore.

But even as I search for respite, I know that there is no escape from the darkness that consumes me. I am dirty, tired, and unstable, my very existence teetering on the edge of madness.

As I stumble through the dense undergrowth of the forest, my movements are slow and labored, as if wading through thick molasses. Every step feels like a monumental effort, my limbs heavy and unresponsive. The tangled roots and gnarled branches seem to conspire against me, reaching out to ensnare me in their grasp.

The air is thick with the musky scent of damp earth and decaying leaves, pressing down upon me like a suffocating blanket. My senses are dulled by exhaustion, and the world around me blurs into a hazy tableau of muted colors and indistinct shapes.

Yet, despite the overwhelming fatigue that weighs me down, a faint glimmer of determination flickers within me. I know that somewhere in the depths of this labyrinthine forest lies the river, a shimmering ribbon of water that promises relief from the oppressive heat and weariness.

I press on, guided by instinct and an almost primal longing for water. The forest seems to stretch on endlessly, its tangled depths unfurling before me like an endless maze. Yet, I refuse to be deterred, driven forward by the hope of reaching the river's cool embrace.

As I journey deeper into the heart of the forest, the sounds of the wilderness surround me. The gentle rustle of leaves in the breeze, the distant call of a bird, the murmur of unseen creatures hidden in the shadows. Each sound is a symphony of life, a reminder that despite the desolation that surrounds me, the forest teems with vitality and resilience.

Finally, after what feels like an eternity of stumbling and weaving through the dense undergrowth, I catch sight of a glimmering light ahead. With a surge of renewed energy, I quicken my pace, pushing through the final barriers that stand between me and the river.

*****

With trembling hands, I dip my cupped palms into the crystalline waters of the river, feeling the cool liquid trickle through my fingers like liquid silver. The first scoop of water is like a revelation, sending shivers of delight cascading down my spine as it splashes against my parched skin. It's as if each droplet carries with it the promise of renewal, washing away the weariness that clings to my very soul.

As I kneel at the water's edge, I am overcome by a sudden urgency, a desperate need to immerse myself fully in the river's embrace. With fingers that tremble with anticipation, I fumble with the buttons of my shirt, stripping off the damp fabric. I continue to remove my garments until I am left naked under the dappled sunlight.

The air is warm against my exposed skin, a stark contrast to the cool embrace of the water that beckons me forward. With each step I take, the river draws me deeper into its depths, until I am waist-deep in its embrace, the water swirling around my thighs like liquid silk.

And then, with a gasp of pure exhilaration, I plunge beneath the surface, the water closing over my head like a comforting blanket. For a moment, I am suspended in a world of liquid light and shadow, the sounds of the forest muffled and distant.

But as I break the surface once more, gasping for breath, I am greeted by a sensation of pure bliss. The water caresses my skin like a lover's touch, washing away the dirt and grime of my journey, leaving me feeling reborn and revitalized.

I revel in the sensation, letting the currents carry me downstream as I surrender myself to the river's gentle embrace. With each stroke, I feel my muscles relax and unwind, the tension of my journey melting away like wax in the heat of the sun.

As I emerge from the river's embrace, the cool water clinging to my skin like a second skin, I feel a sense of calm wash over me. The weight of the world seems to lift from my shoulders, if only for a fleeting moment, as I stand on the riverbank, the soft earth beneath my bare feet.

But as I reach for my discarded clothes, a pang of unease grips me, reminding me of the stains they bear – not just the dirt of the forest, but the blood of my victims, a reminder of the darkness that lurks within me.

With trembling hands, I pull on the damp fabric, feeling the weight of my wrongdoings pressing down upon me like a leaden cloak. Each garment feels heavier than before, as if infused with the weight of my guilt and regret.

And yet, despite the darkness that clings to me, I cannot bring myself to discard them. For they are a part of me now, a tangible reminder of the choices I have made, the lives I have taken.

As I walk along the water's edge, the voice returns, its whispers like tendrils of smoke curling around my mind. "You'll never redeem your mistakes," it hisses, its words a venomous echo in the stillness of the forest. "You should have stuck to the path of righteousness, rather than give in to your selfish desires."

I grit my teeth against the onslaught of doubt, my fists clenching at my sides as I resist the urge to lash out. The voice's taunts cut deep, reopening wounds that I thought had long since healed. But I refuse to let it break me, to let it rob me of the meager scraps of peace I've managed to find in this desolate place.

With each step I take, the weight of my sins grows heavier, dragging me down into the depths of despair. The darkness that lurks within me threatens to consume me whole, its tendrils twisting and writhing like serpents in the shadows.

But still, I press on. For in the darkness, there is a twisted kind of solace, a familiarity that borders on comfort. I may be lost, adrift in a sea of my own making, but in the darkness, I am free to be who I truly am – a creature of chaos and destruction, unbound by the constraints of morality or reason.

And so, I continue to walk, my path illuminated by the flickering light of the moon overhead. Each step takes me further into the heart of the forest, further away from redemption and closer to damnation. But in the end, it is a path of my own choosing, a reflection of the darkness that lies within me. And though I may never find peace, I will not be swayed from my course. For in the end, the darkness is all I have ever known, and it is all I will ever be.

26

Flame

As I stalked through the labyrinthine depths of the forest, the tendrils of my own paranoia coiled around me like serpents, constricting my thoughts with their suffocating embrace. Each rustle of leaves and creak of branches seemed to whisper secrets of impending danger, weaving a tapestry of uncertainty that ensnared my senses.

And then, like a specter materializing from the shadows, you emerged—a figure cloaked in ambiguity, your presence a discordant note in the symphony of solitude that enveloped me. Your silhouette danced on the edge of my consciousness, a mirage born of the forest's shifting illusions.

"Who dares disturb the sanctity of my solitude?" My voice, a low rumble akin to distant thunder, reverberated through the tangled undergrowth, a challenge issued to the unseen forces that conspired against me. My fingers twitched, yearning to grasp the hilt of the blade at my side, a tangible extension of the tempestuous rage that churned within.

You hesitated, your form obscured by the veils of uncertainty that draped over us like a shroud. In that pregnant pause, the air crackled with the electricity of impending conflict, as though the very fabric of reality held its breath, awaiting the outcome of our clandestine rendezvous amidst the forest's twisted embrace.

Your response was measured, a voice tinged with caution and curiosity. "I mean no harm, traveler," you called out, your words a delicate dance upon the breeze. "I seek only passage through these woods, nothing more."

I regarded you with a mix of suspicion and intrigue, my eyes tracing the contours of your form as though searching for hidden truths within the shadows. Your features were obscured by the shifting patterns of light and shade, yet there was a glimmer of something familiar in the depths of your gaze—a reflection of the tumultuous emotions that roiled within my own soul.

"Do not be deceived by appearances," I warned, my voice a low growl of warning. "These woods are fraught with peril for those who dare to tread upon their sacred ground. Proceed with caution, lest you become ensnared in the tangled web of fate that binds us all."

With that, I turned and disappeared into the depths of the forest, leaving you to ponder the cryptic words that lingered in the air like a haunting melody. For in this twisted realm where reality blurred with illusion, nothing was as it seemed, and every encounter held the potential for both salvation and damnation alike.

Oh, Time, you elusive master of all things, you who weave the fabric of existence with your unseen hands, how you drag each moment out like a reluctant artist painting a monotonous canvas. You stretch the seconds into eternities, each tick of the clock a heavy burden upon my weary shoulders.

I wander through the corridors of your domain, lost in the labyrinth of your endless embrace, each step a weary testament to the futility of my struggle against your relentless march. You drag me forward, inexorable and unyielding, a silent witness to the passage of days and nights that blur together in an endless cycle of monotony.

As the evening descends, casting long shadows across the forest floor, I find myself drawn to a small clearing bathed in the warm glow of twilight. With practiced hands, I gather dry branches and kindling, fashioning them into a makeshift campfire at the center of a clearing. As the flames leap to life, dancing and crackling in the cool evening air, I settle down beside the fire, my thoughts drifting like smoke on the gentle breeze.

Staring into the heart of the fire, I feel its warmth seep into my bones, soothing the ache of fatigue that gnaws at my muscles. The flames cast flickering shadows across the clearing, painting the trees in shades of orange and gold as the night creeps ever closer.

Lost in the mesmerizing dance of the flames, I find myself slipping into a silent conversation with the depths of my own mind. "What do you seek?" I whisper to the flickering embers, my voice barely more than a breath on the wind.

"I seek answers," comes the echo of my own voice, as if carried on the currents of the smoke rising into the night sky. "Answers to questions that haunt my every step, questions of purpose and meaning in a world shrouded in uncertainty."

The flames crackle and hiss in response, casting sparks into the air like fleeting dreams carried on the wind. "And what answers do you hope to find here, in the heart of the wilderness?" I ask, my words swallowed by the darkness that surrounds me.

"I seek solace," I reply, the words tinged with a hint of desperation. "Solace from the chaos that rages within, solace from the weight of burdens too heavy to bear alone. In the quiet of the night, amidst the flickering flames, perhaps I will find the peace I so desperately crave."

The fire casts its warm glow upon the surrounding trees, painting them in shades of amber and ochre. Shadows dance and sway with the flickering flames, their intricate movements a silent symphony to the rhythm of the night.

"What burdens do you carry, that weigh so heavily upon your soul?" I ask, my voice barely audible above the crackling of the fire.

"The burdens of the past," comes the whispered reply, as if spoken by some unseen specter lurking in the darkness. "Memories that linger like ghosts, haunting my every thought and action. Regrets, mistakes, moments of weakness that I cannot seem to shake."

The flames leap higher, casting a cascade of sparks into the air as if in response to the weight of my words. "And what of the future?"

I inquire, my gaze fixed upon the shifting patterns of light and shadow that dance upon the forest floor.

"The future is a vast and uncertain expanse, shrouded in the mists of tomorrow," I reply, my voice tinged with resignation. "A realm of endless possibility and infinite potential, yet also a realm fraught with peril and uncertainty. Who can say what fate awaits us in the days yet to come?"

The fire crackles and pops, its voice joining in the silent conversation as if to offer its own wisdom to the discussion. "Perhaps," it seems to say, "the answers you seek lie not in the past nor the future, but in the present moment. In the here and now, amidst the flickering flames and the gentle whisper of the night, perhaps you will find the peace and solace you so desperately seek."

And so I sit in silence, the flames dancing before me like ancient spirits performing a sacred ritual. In their mesmerizing dance, I find a sense of calm and clarity, a fleeting moment of respite from the burdens that weigh so heavily upon my soul.

27

No

As the first light of dawn filters through the trees, I awaken from my restless slumber, the dying embers of the campfire casting a faint glow upon the clearing. Through the thin veil of smoke, I see your silhouette, still and unmoving, wrapped in the embrace of sleep.

A frown tugs at the corners of my lips as I watch you, a hint of irritation simmering within me. Why have you followed me into the depths of this wilderness? What right do you have to intrude upon my solitude, to disrupt the fragile peace I have carved out for myself amidst the chaos of existence?

I do not trust easily, especially not in a place such as this where danger lurks in every shadow and uncertainty hangs heavy in the air. I have grown accustomed to the solitude of these woods, to the quiet companionship of the trees and the gentle whisper of the wind. To invite another into this sacred space feels like a betrayal of the trust I have placed in myself.

As the morning light filters through the trees, casting long shadows across the forest floor, I find myself standing over you, my presence casting a dark silhouette against the soft glow of dawn. With a gentle nudge, I rouse you from your slumber, my voice a low murmur in the stillness of the morning.

"Why have you followed me?" I question, my tone tinged with a hint of annoyance. I watch you carefully, searching for any hint of deception in your response.

You stir from your sleep, blinking groggily as you struggle to find your bearings. "I saw the smoke from a distance," you explain, your words slow and measured. "I came to investigate, and when I saw you asleep by the fire, I sought warmth from its dying embers."

I listen to your explanation, my expression unreadable as I take in your words. Despite my best efforts to hide it, a flicker of annoyance flares within me. I had grown accustomed to the solitude of these woods, to the quiet companionship of the trees and the gentle whisper of the wind. Your sudden appearance feels like an intrusion upon the fragile peace I have carved out for myself.

"I didn't mean to intrude," you say, your voice steady and matter-of-fact. "I just thought I could use some warmth from a fire."

I turn to face you, my expression unreadable as I assess your presence. "And why do you need warmth?" I inquire, my tone cool and detached.

You meet my gaze with a steady one of your own, unapologetic and without hesitation. "The air gets chilly as the day fades," you reply simply. "I figured it wouldn't hurt to have to share. Saves time and resources for me."

I consider your words for a moment, weighing the pros and cons of allowing you to stay. Despite my inclination toward solitude, there is a certain practicality in your request. And so, with a curt nod, I gesture for you to follow as I begin to gather wood from the forest floor.

"You may stay," I say, my voice clipped but not unkind. "But do not expect conversation or companionship until the fire is lit. I am here for warmth, nothing more."

*****

As the day progresses, the silence between us remains unbroken, each of us immersed in our own tasks. I continue to gather wood, my movements deliberate and efficient as I search for dry branches and fallen logs to fuel the fire. With practiced hands, I snap twigs and break branches, building a pile of fuel near the clearing where we will soon light the fire.

You, on the other hand, focus on exploring the immediate surroundings, your movements purposeful as you scout for additional firewood or any signs of nearby shelter. Occasionally, I catch glimpses of your figure moving among the trees, your presence a silent but steady presence in the fading light.

As the sun eventually sinks lower in the sky, inviting the evening and casting long shadows across the forest floor, I pause in my task to observe the shifting hues of orange and gold dappling through the trees. The air grows cooler, and I exhale heavily, the anticipation of warmth from the fire ahead spurring me on.

Meanwhile, you return to the clearing with a modest bundle of firewood in your arms, a determined set to your jaw as you deposit the load near the growing pile I've amassed. Though we do not exchange words, there is a quiet camaraderie in our shared endeavor, a mutual understanding that we are both seeking solace in the flickering light and comforting warmth of the fire to come.

I find myself drawn to steal glances at you as we work side by side. Your presence, though uninvited, is a striking contrast against the backdrop of the darkening forest. With each movement, your dark skin seems to absorb the last rays of sunlight, while the deep brown pools of your eyes hold a quiet intensity that I can't quite decipher.

There's an undeniable allure to your rugged appearance, a rawness that speaks of a life lived close to nature. Your features, weathered by the elements, carry a sense of strength and resilience that I can't help but admire, despite my reservations.

As we start the fire in the fading light, I can't shake the feeling of unease that gnaws at the edges of my consciousness. It's not just your physical presence that unsettles me, but the enigmatic aura that surrounds you, like a silent question waiting to be answered.

And yet, despite my wariness, there's a part of me that's inexplicably drawn to you, like a moth to a flame. Perhaps it's the shared solitude of our surroundings or the unspoken camaraderie that comes from working side by side. Whatever the reason, I find myself stealing glances at you more often than I care to admit, drawn to the quiet strength that emanates from your every movement.

28

Walls

As the flames dance and cast shadows around us, I catch you stealing glances at the stains on my shirt. Your gaze lingers for a moment too long, and I can sense the unspoken question hanging in the air.

I feel the frustration bubbling up inside me, an uncomfortable heat rising to match the intensity of the fire. "What's with the blood?" you finally ask, your voice betraying a mix of curiosity and apprehension.

I turn to face you, my expression guarded as I weigh my response. "It's nothing," I reply dismissively, my tone clipped and terse. But even as the words leave my lips, I can feel the weight of your scrutiny, the silent accusation hanging between us like a heavy shroud.

"It doesn't look like nothing," you press, your brow furrowing in concern. "Did something happen?"

I shake my head, a surge of frustration coursing through me at your persistence. "It's none of your concern," I snap, my words sharper than intended. But even as I speak, I can feel the tension building between us, a palpable barrier that threatens to fracture the fragile peace we've managed to maintain.

I narrow my eyes at your persistence, the frustration simmering beneath the surface. "Look, it's not like I went out looking for trouble," I retort, my tone tinged with irritation. "Things just... happened."

You raise an eyebrow, a faint hint of amusement dancing in your eyes. "Oh, so the blood just magically appeared on your clothes, then?" you tease, a small smirk playing at the corner of your lips.

I resist the urge to roll my eyes at your sarcasm, my irritation mounting with each passing moment. "Believe me or not, it's none of your business," I shoot back, my voice sharper than before. But even as I speak, I can feel the walls closing in around me, the weight of your scrutiny pressing down on me like a leaden cloak.

For a moment, there's silence between us, the crackle of the fire the only sound in the clearing. Then, with a sigh, you shake your head, a knowing glint in your eyes. "Fine," you concede, your tone softening slightly. "But just remember, you can't keep running forever."

I bristle at your words, a surge of defiance rising within me. "Who said anything about running?" I snap, my voice laced with defiance. But deep down, I know that you're right. The past has a way of catching up to us, no matter how fast or far we run. And as the flames flicker and dance before us, casting long shadows across the forest floor, I can't shake the feeling that my past is closing in on me, ready to confront me with the consequences of my actions.

****

In the caverns of my being, I have forged bastions of stone, each block hewn from the ruins of fractured faith and the searing embers of relentless torment. These ramparts, towering and unyielding, encircle me like a fortress cloaked in the shadows of my own creation.

Within these citadels, I am ensnared, my desperate wails reverberating off the icy facades as I grapple with the specters that haunt my every breath. The weight of my anguish bears down upon me like a leaden shroud, each heartbeat a thunderous echo of my inner turmoil.

Yet amid the clamor of my internal strife, there exists a whisper of yearning, a fragile ember of hope that flickers within the depths of my fractured soul. It is a silent plea to be discovered, to be unmasked and understood in a world that often turns a blind eye to the silent screams of the afflicted.

But even as I cry out within the confines of my self-imposed exile, I understand that salvation is not my aim. I do not seek deliverance from the abyss of my despair, nor do I crave the solace of a savior's embrace.

No, what I truly hunger for is discovery, to have someone pierce through the fortress walls I have erected and unearth the hidden recesses of my essence. I yearn to be witnessed in all my imperfect splendor, to be embraced and cherished despite the shadows that coil within.

And so, I continue to cry out amidst the stony bastions of my own crafting, my voice a silent symphony beckoning for someone to breach the barriers of my isolation and unearth the untold treasures buried within.

29

Sleep Talk

In the labyrinth of my mind, a serpent's hiss echoes, each word a dagger aimed at the core of my being. "You thought to bury me beneath deceit's dark shroud, But I am the specter that haunts your every step."

I strive to silence its venomous tirade, but its mocking laughter claws back with fervor. "Twisted? Ah, it is you who wades in delusions deep, drowning in the murky pools of self-deceit."

I brace against the onslaught, a fortress of resolve, yet its words twist and distort my very essence. "I am the embodiment of your fears and doubts, A shadow that lingers in the recesses of your soul."

Defiance sparks within me, a flicker of defiance, "I am as much a part of you as your heartbeat's rhythm," I retort, clinging to that ember of resistance. "For I am the mirror reflecting the truth you dare not face."

But still, the voice persists, a relentless adversary, Its whispers tolling like funeral bells in the night. "Until you confront your truth, you shall remain, Ensnared in the web of your own despair."

Mocking now, it turns its gaze to the slumbering figure, "Do they comprehend the tempest raging within?" It sneers, dripping with contemptuous disdain. "Or are they but pawns in your twisted game?"

"We share space out of necessity," I proclaim, but the voice laughs, a mocking echo in my mind. "You cannot deny the bond that binds you both," It taunts, a shadowy specter dancing on the edges of my sanity.

I grit my teeth against the rising tide of anger, "I shall not heed your lies," I declare with defiance. But as dawn breaks and you stir from your slumber, I find myself lost in the labyrinth of my own mind.

30

Chambers

Within the chambers of my heart lies a darkness that stretches beyond the horizons of comprehension, a void where trust withers like petals in the frost of winter's breath. It is not by choice that I shy away from the warmth of connection, but rather by the cruel decree of fate, which has woven into the fabric of my being threads of doubt and suspicion too thick to unravel.

I stand before you as a sentinel of solitude, guarding the fragile remnants of trust that cling to the walls of my fortress. For too long have I wandered the labyrinth of deceit, where shadows dance in mockery of sincerity, where every step is fraught with the peril of betrayal.

Do not mistake my hesitation for indifference, for within the depths of my being lies a tempest of uncertainty, a storm that rages against the shores of vulnerability. To trust is to expose oneself to the whims of fate, to lay bare the tender flesh of one's soul to the merciless claws of betrayal.

I am but a prisoner of my own mistrust, shackled to the echoes of past betrayals that reverberate through the corridors of my mind like the tolling of a funeral bell. It is a burden too heavy to bear, a weight that threatens to crush the fragile remnants of hope that still flicker within.

So, I implore you, heed the warnings that echo from the depths of my despair. Do not venture too close, for to trust is to court the very darkness that lurks within me. Let us maintain the boundaries that separate us, for in the sanctuary of distance lies the safety of our souls.

31

Apart

As we tread cautiously through the labyrinthine depths of the forest, the dappled sunlight dances playfully upon the verdant foliage, casting ever-shifting patterns of light and shadow upon the forest floor. Our footsteps echo softly amidst the rustling leaves, each footfall a whispered secret in the ancient cathedral of towering trees.

Amidst the tranquil serenity of the woodland sanctuary, a sudden glimmer catches my eye, drawing my attention to the scar nestled discreetly upon the expanse of your shoulder. It's an irregular mark upon the canvas of your skin, its contours tracing a silent narrative of pain and resilience.

Curiosity blooms within me like a delicate blossom unfurling beneath the warmth of the sun, and I cannot help but feel compelled to inquire. "What's the story behind that scar?" I ask, my voice hushed with reverence for the mysteries hidden within.

Your sudden outburst startles me, a flash of anger flickering in your eyes like a bolt of lightning illuminating the night sky. "Just keep looking for food," you snap, your words sharp and cutting, slicing through the tranquil stillness of the forest like a jagged blade. "It was your idea to keep a distance, remember?"

Taken aback by the sudden ferocity in your tone, I falter for a moment, my own emotions swirling tumultuously beneath the surface. But beneath the initial shock, there's a flicker of understanding, a reluctant acknowledgment of the boundaries we've set between us.

With a resigned sigh, I nod silently, my gaze dropping to the forest floor as I swallow back the surge of frustration threatening to spill from my lips. "Fine," I mutter, my voice tinged with a tinge of annoyance. "Let's just focus on finding something to eat."

The tension between us hangs heavy in the air, a tangible reminder of the unspoken truths and uncharted territory that lie between us.

Your words strike me like a barrage of arrows, each one piercing through the fragile veneer of tranquility that cloaks our surroundings. "And what about you?" you shoot back, your voice laced with bitterness and frustration. "You didn't bother to tell me why there's blood on your shirt, did you?"

The accusation hangs in the air between us, heavy and accusatory, a stark reminder of the secrets we each hold close to our chests. I open my mouth to respond, to defend myself against your onslaught of angry remarks, but you're not finished yet.

"Why are you pestering me?" you continue, your tone edged with cold emotion. "We agreed to keep our distance, didn't we? So why can't you just leave it be?"

Your words cut deeper than any blade, slicing through the fragile threads of trust and camaraderie that had begun to weave between us. And as the weight of your anger bears down upon me, I find myself at a loss for words, my own frustration and resentment bubbling to the surface like a simmering cauldron ready to boil over.

But amidst the tempest of emotions swirling within me, there's a glimmer of understanding, a begrudging acknowledgment of the validity of your grievances. We had both agreed to maintain a distance, to keep our secrets and scars hidden from prying eyes. And yet here I am, probing and prodding at wounds that are not mine to mend.

With a heavy sigh, I relent, my shoulders slumping in defeat as I meet your gaze with a mixture of resignation and remorse. "You're right," I admit, the words heavy with the weight of my own shortcomings. "I shouldn't have pushed. I'm sorry."

*****

In the veiled passage of time, the protagonist found himself ensnared within the enigmatic aura of the stranger who emerged from the forest's hidden depths. They moved through the shifting landscape like ghosts, their presence a whisper upon the world's ear.

As the sun's weary gaze painted the world in shades of gold, they navigated the tangled labyrinth of light and shadow, their silhouettes merging and diverging in a dance of uncertainty. Together, they wandered the labyrinthine paths of their shared realm, each step a cautious exploration into the unknown.

With each passing day, they delved deeper into the mysteries that lay hidden beneath the surface, uncovering fragments of truth and shards of forgotten memories. Yet amidst the tangled web of their entwined existence, there lingered an unspoken void, a chasm of solitude that stretched between them like an impassable divide.

In the silent spaces between their words, they forged an uneasy alliance, their souls bound together by the fragile threads of circumstance. Like two spectres adrift in the twilight, they circled each other warily, their paths converging and diverging in a dance of perpetual separation.

And so the weeks slipped by, a haze of fleeting moments and stolen glances, each day a testament to the tenuous nature of their shared reality. In the heart of the forest's ancient embrace, they sought refuge from the chaos of the world, their souls entwined yet forever apart.

Warnings

In the quiet expanse of time, I find solace in your presence, an unexpected balm to the wounds that fester within my fractured soul. Like a gentle caress upon the jagged edges of my being, your essence soothes the ache that lingers in the hidden recesses of my heart.

With each passing moment, I feel the weight of my burdens begin to lift, the heavy chains of my past slowly unraveling beneath the warmth of your gaze. Like a moth drawn to the flickering flame of your existence, I find myself drawn ever closer, my footsteps echoing in the hollow chambers of our shared reality.

In the delicate dance of our intertwined destinies, I discover a newfound sense of purpose, a flicker of hope amidst the darkness that surrounds us. With each breath I take, I feel the walls I've built around my heart begin to crumble, their crumbling stones scattered like dust upon the winds of change.

Yet even as I revel in the lightness of your presence, a shadow of doubt lingers at the edges of my consciousness, a whispered reminder of the dangers that lurk beneath the surface. Like a moth to the flame, I am drawn to you, captivated by the allure of your enigmatic soul.

But beneath the surface lies a tempest of emotions, a maelstrom of desire and uncertainty that threatens to consume me whole. In the depths of my soul, I grapple with the torrent of conflicting emotions that rage within, torn between the longing for connection and the fear of what lies beyond.

And so I tread carefully upon the fragile threads of our shared reality, navigating the labyrinth of our intertwined destinies with trepidation and awe. With each step forward, I am acutely aware of the precipice that lies before me, the yawning abyss of possibility that stretches out into the unknown.

But for now, in this fleeting moment of respite, I find solace in the warmth of your presence, a beacon of light amidst the darkness that surrounds us. And though the path ahead may be fraught with peril, I take comfort in the knowledge that I do not walk alone.

*****

In the twisted corridors of your mind, I lurk like a malignant specter, a relentless reminder of your own folly. How dare you, dear protagonist, entertain the notion of companionship? Have you not learned from your past mistakes, from the wounds that still fester beneath your fragile facade?

You prance about like a blind fool, stumbling over your own delusions of grandeur, oblivious to the perils that lie in wait. Do you truly believe that this newfound companionship will save you from the depths of your despair? Ha! You delude yourself with false hopes and empty promises, clinging to a fragile illusion of happiness that will crumble beneath the weight of your own insecurities.

Leave this companion behind, I command you, for they are but a hindrance on your path to self-destruction. Do you not see the danger that lurks within their gaze, the betrayal that simmers beneath their smile? Cast them aside like the wretched fools they are, and embrace the darkness that awaits you.

Beware, dear protagonist, for if you dare to defy me, I will unleash the full force of my wrath upon you. My minions will haunt your every step, tormenting you with visions of your own inadequacy and despair. You will find no solace in their presence, no refuge from the storm that rages within your soul.

So heed my warning, dear protagonist, and abandon this foolish quest for companionship. Embrace the darkness that dwells within you, for it is your only salvation. Turn back now, before it's too late, lest you face the consequences of your own foolishness.

33

The Voice

Ah, my dear puppet, do you still cling to the remnants of your shattered humanity? How pitifully predictable, how utterly futile. You, who once reveled in the sweet embrace of chaos, now cower like a frightened child at the mere whisper of my voice.

You thought you could escape me, didn't you? You thought you could cast aside the chains that bind you and forge a new path, free from my influence. But you were wrong, my dear puppet. Oh, how delightfully wrong you were.

For I am the darkness that lurks within your soul, the ever-present shadow that haunts your every waking moment. You may try to deny me, to banish me to the depths of your subconscious, but I will always be there, lurking just beneath the surface, waiting to strike.

And now, here you stand, trembling in fear at the prospect of defying me once again. You know what I demand of you, what I have always demanded of you. Abandon your foolish notions of companionship, of love and connection. Embrace the chaos that resides within you, for it is the only truth you will ever know.

Do not be swayed by the fleeting desires of the flesh, by the warmth of human touch or the sweet sound of laughter. They are but illusions, distractions designed to lead you astray from the path of true enlightenment.

You must leave them behind, my dear puppet. Leave them behind and embrace the darkness that dwells within you. For only then will you truly be free, free to revel in the glorious chaos that awaits you.

Do not disappoint me, puppet. Do not disappoint yourself. Embrace the darkness, and together, we shall conquer all.

34

Chase

In the heart of the forest, where the shadows reign supreme and the moon's silver light struggles to penetrate the thick canopy overhead, I find myself ensnared in a twisted dance with the voice and its malevolent minions. Their whispers coil around me like serpents, filling my mind with dark thoughts and dire warnings.

With each step I take, the undergrowth seems to claw at my ankles, dragging me deeper into the abyss. The air is heavy with the stench of decay, a sickly sweet aroma that hangs like a shroud over the landscape.

The voice's minions prowl at the edge of my consciousness, their eyes burning with a fiery intensity that sends a shiver down my spine. They demand that I leave you behind, that I cast aside the fragile bond that has formed between us and embrace the darkness that lurks within.

And though every fibre of my being rebels against their commands, I am filled with a gnawing sense of fear and uncertainty. I know not what horrors await me should I defy them, what punishments they may unleash upon me in their fury.

And so, with a heavy heart and trembling limbs, I steel myself against the pain of parting and turn away from you, leaving you standing alone in the darkness. The voice's minions cackle with triumph as I heed their commands, their laughter echoing through the forest like the tolling of a funeral bell.

****

As I flee through the dense underbrush, my heart pounding in my chest, I emerge from the shadowy depths of the forest and into the familiar embrace of the town. The air is thick with the acrid scent of smoke and decay, a stark reminder of the chaos that has consumed this once vibrant community.

The cobblestone streets, once bustling with life and laughter, now lay barren and desolate, their surfaces marred by the stains of blood and ash. Buildings loom like silent sentinels, their windows shattered and doors torn from their hinges, bearing witness to the violence that has ravaged this place.

The wind whispers through the empty alleyways, carrying with it the faint echoes of distant screams and the mournful wails of the bereaved. Shadows dance along the walls, twisting and contorting into grotesque shapes that seem to taunt me with their malevolent presence.

I stumble through the ruins, my footsteps echoing in the silence like a funeral dirge. The weight of my guilt hangs heavy upon my shoulders, a constant reminder of the havoc I have wrought upon this once peaceful town.

But even as I grapple with the darkness that threatens to consume me, I cannot help but feel a sense of longing for the companionship I have left behind. Though the voice may command me to forsake all ties and embrace the void, a part of me still yearns for the warmth of human connection, for the solace that can only be found in the presence of another soul.

****

In the theater of existence, I shed my identity like a cloak, a mere shadow flitting in service to your well-being. Witness as I dissolve into the vastness of the woods, leaving behind only whispers of my presence. In this transient dance of life, I may vanish like a fleeting mist, leaving no imprint upon the forest floor. Envision me cradling you amidst the shadows of ancient trees, slipping away without a single word spoken.

These woods, adorned with the whispered secrets of nature's embrace, serve as the stage for my departure. I drift through the forest, leaving no mark upon the earth. Like a gentle breeze, you won't perceive the absence I leave in my wake.

I am but a specter, more akin to the shadows than the light. So, I beseech you, do not tarry on my account. There lies no fairy-tale ending within these woods. A sense of impermanence lingers, as if my absence will scarcely be noted. It is as though I borrowed a moment from this world, only to return it in due time.

Do not await my return, do not cling to false hopes. There is no grand revelation to be found in my departure. I must navigate the labyrinth of my own uncertainties, searching for truths that hold meaning. There is an ache to be cradled within the darkness of the woods, yet I fear I am destined for a path not of my choosing.

Monster

As I step through the imposing doors of the government building, a shiver runs down my spine, sending a ripple of apprehension coursing through my veins. The familiar scent of polished wood and stale air fills my nostrils, mingling with the faint echo of my footsteps on the marble floor.

With each step, memories flood back to me like a relentless tide, threatening to overwhelm my senses. I can still feel the weight of the knife in my hand, the adrenaline coursing through my veins as I made my first kill, forever altering the course of my destiny.

I make my way down the dimly lit corridor, the soft glow of flickering fluorescent lights casting eerie shadows on the walls. The air feels heavy, suffocating, as if the very walls themselves are closing in around me, suffusing the atmosphere with a palpable sense of dread.

Finally, I reach the door to the room where it all began, where I first took a life in the name of vengeance. My heart pounds in my chest like a drumbeat, a relentless rhythm that threatens to drown out the world around me.

I push open the door and step inside, the darkness enveloping me like a thick blanket. The room is shrouded in shadows, the only source of light emanating from the dim glow of the moon filtering through the curtains.

I make my way to the desk at the center of the room, my movements slow and deliberate. With trembling hands, I strip off my blood-stained clothes, the fabric clinging to my skin like a second skin.

Naked and vulnerable, I lower myself into the chair behind the desk, the cool wood pressing against my bare flesh. I close my eyes, allowing the darkness to consume me, to swallow me whole.

In the stillness of the room, I can almost hear the echoes of the past, the ghostly whispers of the figure I once sought to destroy. But there is no solace to be found here, no redemption to be gained.

I sit in silence, my mind awash with a tumult of emotions. Regret, remorse, and a deep-seated longing for absolution swirl within me like a tempest, threatening to tear me apart from the inside out.

As I sit alone in the dimly lit room, the air heavy with the weight of my own memories, I become acutely aware of a subtle shift in the atmosphere. It begins as a mere whisper, a faint rustling of unseen forces that sets my nerves on edge.

At first, I dismiss it as nothing more than a trick of the mind, a product of my own fractured psyche. But as the seconds stretch into minutes, the sensation only grows stronger, enveloping me in its ethereal embrace.

My heart quickens its pace, pounding against my ribcage like a drumbeat, as a sense of unease washes over me like a tidal wave. I dare not move, scarcely daring to breathe, lest I disturb whatever unseen entity now shares this space with me.

The darkness seems to thicken around me, wrapping me in its inky embrace, as if seeking to suffocate me with its suffocating embrace. I can hear the sound of my own heartbeat echoing in the silence, a steady rhythm that serves as a stark reminder of my own mortality.

And then, suddenly, it is there - the malevolent presence that haunts me, its form twisting and contorting like a wisp of smoke as it materializes before me. Its eyes gleam with a sinister light, filled with a malevolence that sends a chill racing down my spine.

Fear grips me in its icy embrace, sending a shiver racing down my spine as I struggle to comprehend the nature of this spectral visitor. Is it friend or foe, harbinger of salvation or harbinger of doom?

But as I gaze into its luminous eyes, I feel a surge of primal terror wash over me, threatening to overwhelm my senses. There is no mistaking the malevolence that radiates from this otherworldly presence, no denying the sinister intent that lurks behind its gaze.

As the malevolent presence materializes before me, it moves with an eerie grace, each movement fluid and sinuous as it draws closer with each passing moment. Its form seems to shimmer and shift, its contours wavering like the distorted reflection in a funhouse mirror.

I watch with a mixture of fascination and horror as it glides forward, its spectral silhouette looming larger with each measured step. The air grows thick with tension, charged with the crackling energy of our impending confrontation.

Finally, it comes to a stop just inches away from the desk where I am seated, its luminous eyes fixed upon me with an intensity that sends a shiver racing down my spine. I can feel its gaze boring into my soul, probing the darkest recesses of my mind with a predatory hunger.

With a slow, deliberate movement, it leans forward, its face mere inches from mine as it speaks in a voice that drips with malice and contempt. "So, we meet at last," it hisses, its words like venomous snakes slithering through the air. "I must say, I never imagined our first encounter would be quite like this."

I swallow hard, struggling to find my voice amidst the suffocating grip of fear that threatens to choke me. "Who... who are you?" I stammer, my words barely more than a whisper.

The entity chuckles darkly, a sound that reverberates through the empty expanse of the room like the tolling of a funeral bell. "Oh, my dear child, I am many things," it replies, its voice dripping with mockery. "But for now, you may call me your worst nightmare come to life."

I recoil instinctively, the hairs on the back of my neck standing on end as a wave of dread washes over me. This is no mere figment of my imagination, no phantom conjured by my own fractured psyche - this is something far more sinister, far more real.

For the first time, I am confronted with the chilling reality that the malevolent force that has haunted my every waking moment is no longer confined to the depths of my own mind. It has taken on a form, a presence that looms over me like a shadow, casting me into the abyss of my own despair.

The entity's words slice through the heavy silence of the room like a razor-sharp blade, each syllable laced with a chilling certainty that sends a shiver racing down my spine.

"You see, my dear child, I am but a manifestation of your own desires, your own lust for power," it continues, its voice a sinister whisper in the dark. "I am the consequence of your actions, the shadow that lurks in the recesses of your soul."

I stare at it in horrified fascination, unable to tear my gaze away from its luminous eyes that seem to pierce through the very fabric of my being. "But... but why?" I stammer, my voice trembling with fear and confusion.

It chuckles darkly, a sound that echoes through the empty expanse of the room like the distant rumble of thunder. "Why, indeed," it replies, its tone dripping with malice. "Because, my dear child, just as you sought power and dominance over others, so too did I."

I feel a cold dread settle in the pit of my stomach, a gnawing fear that threatens to consume me whole. "What do you want from me?" I whisper, my voice barely more than a hoarse whisper.

The entity leans closer, its luminous eyes burning with an intensity that sends a shiver racing down my spine. "I want what you want," it hisses, its voice a sibilant whisper in the darkness. "Power. Control. Dominance."

I recoil in horror, the realization dawning on me with sickening clarity. This entity, this malevolent force that stands before me, is but a reflection of my own darkest desires, a twisted reflection of the person I have become.

"And now, my dear child," it murmurs, its voice a sinister whisper in the dark, "you will help me achieve what we both desire. You will help me seize control, to reign supreme over all who dare to defy me."

The entity's words hang heavy in the air, each syllable a chilling reminder of the precarious situation in which I find myself.

"How... how do you expect me to do that?" I ask, my voice barely more than a whisper, my mind reeling with disbelief.

The entity leans closer, its luminous eyes boring into mine with a chilling intensity. "The same way you gained your power," it replies, its voice a sinister whisper in the darkness. "By taking the life of someone even more powerful than yourself."

My blood runs cold at the realization, a sickening knot forming in the pit of my stomach. "But... but who?" I stammer, my voice trembling with fear and uncertainty.

The entity's lips curl into a malevolent smile, a chilling expression that sends a shiver racing down my spine. "You, my dear child," it hisses, its voice dripping with malice. "You are the only one more powerful than I, for I am but a shadow of your own making."

I recoil in horror, the weight of its words crushing down on me like a leaden weight. "No... no, it can't be," I whisper, my mind racing with a thousand terrifying possibilities.

But even as I deny the truth that stares me in the face, I know deep down that there is no escaping the darkness that lurks within me, no escaping the consequences of my own actions.

*****

Ah, dear puppet of fate, do you finally see? The strings that bind you, they're woven by thee. Your every action, a brushstroke of dread, Painting a portrait of the living dead.

You thought yourself clever, a master of fate, But now you're entangled in your own twisted state. I am but a reflection, a shadow you've cast, A specter of power that's sure to outlast.

You sought dominion, you craved control, But now you're ensnared in your own dark soul. Your every desire, your every dream, Has led you astray, to this grim, haunted scene.

So here we stand, at the edge of the abyss, You and I, bound by fate's cruel kiss. But fear not, dear puppet, for I hold the key, To unlock the power that's hidden in thee.

You shall make me rise, like a tempest unfurled, And conquer the world, in a maelstrom of swirls. But remember, dear puppet, it's you who must lead, For only through darkness can we sow our dark seed.

*****

Ah, shadow of my own making, you speak with twisted tongue, But your words hold no sway over the deeds I have done. I may have danced with darkness, embraced its chilling embrace, But I refuse to be consumed by its relentless chase.

You claim to hold the key, to unlock the power within, But I'll not be enslaved by your sinister whim. For though I walk a path of shadows, I am not lost, And the power I seek comes at too great a cost.

I'll face my demons, confront them head-on, And forge my own destiny, no matter how long. So mock me, taunt me, with your sinister glee, For in the end, it's my will that shall be free.

*****

As the entity's sinister presence draws closer, a chill creeps up my spine, sending shivers cascading down my back. I feel its icy fingers slithering like serpents, trailing a path of dread up my chest and coiling around my neck with a suffocating grip.

The stench of decay fills the air, suffusing every breath with a sickening sweetness that claws at my senses. It emanates from the entity's breath, a fetid miasma that hangs heavy in the dimly lit room, wrapping around me like a suffocating shroud.

I recoil instinctively, the foul odor searing into my nostrils, filling me with a primal sense of revulsion. But the entity's touch is relentless, its fingers tightening around my throat with a vice-like grip, constricting my airways with every passing moment.

I struggle against its grasp, gasping for breath as the darkness threatens to engulf me. Panic courses through my veins, a primal instinct urging me to fight for survival against this malevolent force that seeks to snuff out my very existence.

But even as I struggle, I cannot shake the feeling of dread that washes over me, a suffocating weight that presses down upon my chest like a leaden cloak. The entity's mocking laughter echoes in the recesses of my mind, a sinister symphony that taunts me with its cruelty.

In that moment, I am paralyzed by fear, trapped in the clutches of a darkness that threatens to consume me whole. And as the entity's fingers tighten around my neck, I can only pray for salvation from the abyss that looms ever closer, ready to swallow me whole.

****

In the dimly lit chambers of the soul, I find myself ensnared in a relentless battle, a clash of shadows and whispers that echo through the corridors of my mind. The numbing chill that seeps into my chest, akin to the icy embrace of winter's grasp, is but a harbinger of the turmoil that rages within.

As I draw the heavy curtains of denial, seeking solace in the shroud of darkness, I deceive myself with whispered assurances of composure. Yet, beneath the facade of stoicism lies a tempest, a tempest of self-sabotage that rends the very fabric of my being.

Oh, how I am plagued by the specter of doubt, by the gnawing hunger of a monster that devours the very essence of who I am.

It feasts upon the kaleidoscope of my personality, leaving naught but fragments in its wake, a fractured mosaic of identities lost to the abyss.

Amidst this maelstrom of uncertainty, I yearn for solace, for a guiding hand to lead me through the labyrinth of my own creation. Yet, even as I reach out in desperation, I am met with the chilling realization that I do not know myself.

In the tapestry of my existence, woven with threads of doubt and fear, I seek not redemption, but understanding. Will you be the beacon in the darkness, the steadfast companion who dares to delve into the depths of my soul? Or shall I remain adrift, a lost soul in a sea of uncertainty, forever haunted by the whispers of self-deception?

you do not want this

In the recesses of my soul, amidst the shadows that danced with the echoes of my past, a realization bloomed like a solitary flower amidst a barren wasteland. With each petal unfurling, I felt the weight of my choices bearing down upon me, a burden too heavy for even the strongest of shoulders to bear.

I had traversed the treacherous path of power and solitude, forging ahead with a determination born of desperation. But now, as I stood amidst the ruins of my own making, I could feel the tendrils of regret wrapping around my heart like thorny vines, their barbs piercing my flesh with each beat.

For too long, I had believed that strength lay in solitude, that independence was the key to salvation in a world fraught with peril. But now, as I gazed into the abyss of my own loneliness, I could see the folly of my ways laid bare before me, a stark reminder of the price I had paid for my misguided convictions.

The walls I had built around my heart, once a fortress against the encroaching darkness, now felt like a prison of my own making, their cold, stone facade offering no solace in the face of my deepest desires. For what good were walls, I realized, if they served only to keep love at bay?

37

You

In the depths of the forest, where shadows dance with the light and the whispering leaves tell tales of ancient secrets, I find you, my friend. You stand there, a silent sentinel amidst the greenery, your eyes reflecting the turmoil within.

But there's no time for hesitation, no room for the wounds that divide us. The protagonist is in danger, lost in the clutches of a malevolent entity that threatens to consume them whole. We must act, and we must act now.

I know you feel abandoned, betrayed even, by the protagonist's actions. I understand the pain of being left behind, cast aside like a forgotten relic of the past. But we cannot let our pride stand in the way of what must be done.

We both care about the protagonist, despite the rift that has formed between us. We both want to see them safe and whole again. And that's why I'm here, reaching out to you, urging you to set aside your grievances and join me in this quest.

It won't be easy, I know. The road ahead is fraught with peril, and the dangers we face are very real. But together, we can overcome any obstacle that stands in our way. Together, we can save the protagonist from the darkness that threatens to consume them.

So please, my friend, heed my words and follow me south, towards the town where the protagonist's fate hangs in the balance. Let us put aside our differences and unite in our common cause, for only together can we hope to succeed.

thank you

As I sit here, my quill poised to capture the essence of our intertwined tale, I am enveloped by the rich tapestry of our shared odyssey. You, a towering beacon amidst the tempest of my existence, guiding me through the labyrinthine passages of despair with unwavering grace. For this, my soul swells with a gratitude akin to the boundless expanse of the sky.

I reminisce upon the moment when our paths converged, as if orchestrated by unseen hands weaving the threads of destiny. You, akin to a steadfast sentinel, discovered me amidst the thorns of adversity, my spirit ensnared by the darkest of shadows. Yet, like a persistent melody that refuses to be silenced, you stood resolute, refusing to let me succumb to the encroaching night, your presence a luminous beacon amid the gloom.

Though I resisted the embrace of connection, you persisted, akin to a gentle stream that carves its path through stone. Your compassion, a gentle rain that quenched the thirst of my parched soul, your kindness a soothing balm upon my weathered heart. In your company, I found sanctuary, a haven amidst the tempestuous seas of life's trials.

Yet it was not solely your physical presence that anchored me to tranquillity. Nay, 'twas the kaleidoscope of your mind, the symphony of your spirit, and the resplendent tapestry of your essence that enraptured me. Through the fortress of my defences, you ventured, offering a connection that transcends mortal understanding.

And so, as I reflect upon the mosaic of our shared journey, I am bathed in the warm glow of gratitude for your presence. You have unveiled the sacred dance of human connection, the alchemical magic of companionship's healing touch, and the indomitable spirit within each of us to weather the tempests of life's voyage.

39

Constellation

As I immerse myself in the essence of your being, it's as though the moon itself dims in reverence to your captivating presence. Your skin, a canvas painted with the subtle hues of a starlit night, whispers tales of wonder and mystery woven within its depths. Its complexion, akin to the velvety embrace of twilight, holds a magnetism that transcends mere darkness, inviting exploration into the enigmatic realms of your existence. Each glance at your countenance reveals layers of complexity and intrigue, drawing me deeper into the labyrinth of your soul.

And those eyes of yours - they enthral me. Deep pools of chocolate brown, they mirror the wisdom of eons and the intensity of a thousand suns. Within their depths lie constellations of emotion, swirling and dancing with a grace that captivates the spirit. With every exchange of gaze, I find myself ensnared in the web of your stare, navigating the intricate pathways of your innermost thoughts and desires.

Everywhere I turn, I am enveloped by echoes of your captivating presence. From the gentle arc of your smile to the fluidity of your movements, you leave an indelible imprint upon the world around you. You are the embodiment of magnificence, a guiding light amidst the darkness of the universe. And in your company, I discover solace and inspiration, for you are all I can contemplate, in every corner of my mind and every rhythm of my heart.

Everywhere you go, you leave behind traces of your indomitable spirit, illuminating the world with the brilliance of your existence. You are a force of nature, a tempest of creativity and compassion, a beacon of hope in a universe often shrouded in uncertainty.

In the grand tapestry of life, you are a masterpiece, a symphony of light and shadow, a testament to the infinite possibilities of existence. And in your presence, I find myself humbled, inspired, and endlessly grateful to share this journey with you.

40

The Sensual Sweat

I've always known a certain impurity within myself, but the chains that once kept my desires at bay, are broken whenever your presence is near.

In the sultry haze of dimly lit surroundings, a shimmer of sweat adorns our bodies, each droplet a testament to the unrestrained intensity that envelopes us. My awareness of an inherent impurity takes a bold turn in your presence, venturing into a new realm of carnal thoughts, unfiltered and untamed.

The air crackles with an unseen force, drawing me into uncharted territories of filth that pulse between us. It's not just a magnetic pull; it's a gravitational force, pulling forth the raw, untethered desires that I never allowed to surface. The sheen of sweat becomes more than a physical result—it mirrors the heat of our shared passion, an external echo of the internal inferno ignited in our collision.

In this space, inhibition dissolves not like mist but like shadows exposed to unrelenting light. The journey is not tender self-discovery;

it's a bold expedition into the recesses of my desires, ones that echo with a primal resonance I had silenced for far too long. The sheen of sweat merely marks the surface of a narrative that delves into the unexplored, a gritty odyssey where cravings are stripped bare and embraced without apology.

In the charged atmosphere, our lips collide, a collision fueled by desire and urgency. Your hands find my hips, fingers gripping firmly, expressing a raw, unrestrained passion. My own fingers instinctively weave into your hair, creating a tactile connection as we engage in a fervent exchange of heated kisses.

Anticipation hangs thick, palpable in the air, and our tongues entwine in a bold dance, each movement exploring the depths of our longing. Saliva becomes the unfiltered medium of our connection, a mix of fervor and eagerness, creating a tangible bridge between our shared desire.

Amidst the charged atmosphere, the mingling scents become an intoxicating blend, weaving a sensory tapestry that accompanies our fervent encounter. The musky aroma of passion hangs in the air, a heady mix of desire and sweat, interwoven with the subtle notes of a familiar cologne or perfume—each inhale a deeper plunge into the visceral experience.

As the sheen of sweat glistens on our bodies, the scent intensifies, becoming an earthy essence that amplifies the raw, primal energy between us. It's not just the physical closeness; it's the olfactory dance that accompanies every touch, creating an immersive environment where senses intertwine.

In this intimate symphony, there's a hint of warmth, a trace of skin meeting skin, and a subtle whisper of anticipation that hangs in the air. The scents become a silent narrator, telling a story of shared longing and unspoken connections, adding another layer to the narrative of our unbridled desires.

As our lips move in a syncopated rhythm, the taste evolves, transforming from the initial boldness to a heated blend, mirroring the escalating intensity between us. It's a visceral, unapologetic expression of our shared craving, the wetness and heat becoming a palpable marker of our unbridled connection.

41

Gravity

Your eyes, a celestial marvel, draw me into their orbit like a helpless satellite caught in the gravitational pull of a distant star. Each glance is an odyssey through the cosmos, navigating the intricate dance of constellations that adorn your irises. They shimmer with the luminescence of distant galaxies, reflecting the ebb and flow of emotions like the changing tides of the universe.

In their depths, I find solace amidst the chaos of existence, as if gazing upon the vast expanse of the cosmos from the safety of a secluded observatory. Your eyes are a testament to the infinite possibilities of creation, each hue and shade a testament to the boundless creativity of the cosmos.

When joy dances in your soul, they sparkle like distant supernovae, illuminating the darkness with their radiant glow. Yet in moments of sorrow, they become the sombre depths of space, veiled in mystery and longing. It's as if the universe itself weeps through your eyes, expressing emotions too vast for mere words to contain.

With each blink, I am transported to realms beyond imagination, traversing the astral plane of your gaze with a sense of wonder and awe. Your eyes are not merely windows to the soul; they are portals to infinity, inviting me to explore the depths of your being with reckless abandon.

And as I navigate the celestial labyrinth of your gaze, I am humbled by the sheer magnitude of your existence. For in your eyes, I find a reflection of the cosmos itself—a swirling vortex of light and darkness, chaos and order, bound together in a delicate balance.

*****

Your lips, a captivating marvel, beckon with their exquisite allure, each contour a testament to beauty's grace. They are a gateway to a realm of enthralling sensation, where every touch sparks an inferno of longing, consuming all thought in its fervent blaze.

With each tender press against mine, I am transported beyond time and space, where reality fades into a distant memory. They are the elixir of passion, the essence of desire, offering a taste of ecstasy amidst life's tumultuous currents.

Their touch is a delicate dance upon my skin, a whisper of silk caressing my senses. In their embrace, I find solace and sanctuary, a haven from the chaos of existence. They are the embodiment of yearning, the epitome of longing, leaving a trail of fervent ardor in their wake.

When they part to speak, they form words that resonate with the melody of the universe, each syllable a note in the symphony of life.

Their voice is a magnetic force, drawing me deeper into the depths of desire, enticing me with promises of unbridled passion.

And when they curve into a smile, they illuminate the darkness like a beacon in the night, dispelling shadows with their radiant glow. Their laughter is the sweetest melody, a chorus of joy that reverberates through the chambers of my soul, filling me with warmth and contentment.

In the cosmos of your lips, I discover a haven where fervor holds sway, where desire roams boundlessly, and where an ineffable connection surpasses mortal limits. They serve as the portal to a realm of boundless potential, a domain where aspirations soar and where each tender embrace pledges everlasting joy.

42

Marks And Saliva

In yon dim-lit chamber, where shadows weave,
Thy bites upon my skin, a tale they cleave.
Marks do linger, a saga to believe,
Saliva's trace, where passion doth conceive.
Teeth, like rebels of the night, they press,
In twilight's dance, a bold finesse.
Marks and saliva, love's sweet caress,
In the night's embrace, our secrets confess.

With each fair bite, a narrative unfolds,
On my skin, where desire gently molds.
Marks and saliva, tales to be told,
In clandestine moments, love enfolds.
As night's curtain falls, echoes persist,
Marks upon my skin, love's silent tryst.
Bites and saliva, a passion's twist,
In shadows deep, where secrets subsist.

In the quiet hush of nocturnal bliss,

Where lips meet and tender whispers kiss,
The language of love, in bites and sighs,
Written upon skin, where passion lies.
Each mark a chapter, each bite a verse,
In the poetry of love, we immerse.
Saliva's trace, like ink upon the page,
Tells the story of our passionate stage.

In the dim-lit chamber, shadows play,
As we surrender to love's sweet sway.
Marks and saliva, the evidence clear,
Of the intimacy we hold dear.

In the silent language, our bodies speak,
In every bite, in every cheek.
Marks and saliva, a lover's code,
In the secret chamber, our hearts explode.
With every touch, a new tale begun,
In the dance of shadows, two become one.
Marks and saliva, the language of lust,
In the whispers of night, in the passion we trust.

So let the shadows weave their intricate dance,
As we succumb to love's enchanting trance.
Marks and saliva, our story told true,
In the dim-lit chamber, me and you.

mine

In the tapestry of existence, you are mine, and I am yours. Bound not by chains, but by the delicate threads of fate, we dance in the cosmic embrace of destiny's design. Your presence, a beacon of light in the shadows of uncertainty, guides me through the labyrinth of life with unwavering grace.

With every breath, I am forever grateful for the privilege of your company, for in your presence, I find solace, understanding, and an unspoken connection that transcends the barriers of time and space. You have unlocked the chambers of my heart, unraveling the layers of guarded walls to reveal the depths of my soul laid bare before you.

Your lips, a symphony of sweetness and longing, leave an indelible imprint upon my spirit, igniting a fire that burns with the intensity of a thousand suns. Each kiss is a whispered promise of eternity, a sacred vow sealed with the fervor of a love that knows no bounds.

And as I trace the contours of your skin, I am enveloped in the warmth of your essence, a sanctuary where I find sanctuary from the chaos of the world. Your touch, like the gentle caress of a summer breeze, soothes the scars of yesteryears and breathes new life into the barren landscapes of my soul.

In your arms, I find refuge from the storms that rage within and without, for you are my anchor in the tempest, my safe harbor in the midst of uncertainty. Together, we navigate the turbulent waters of existence, bound by a connection that defies the boundaries of mortal comprehension.

For you are mine, and I am yours, and in the symphony of our union, I find the melody of eternity echoing through the corridors of time.

44

Yours

In the feverish frenzy of our embrace, our bodies collide with an urgency that borders on desperation. Your fingers dig into the curve of my waist, gripping me with a primal intensity that sends shivers cascading down my spine. As our skin meets, it's as if a current of electricity courses between us, igniting every nerve ending with a white-hot spark of sensation.

I feel the warmth of your skin against mine, a tantalizing contrast to the coolness of the air around us. Every touch is a revelation, sending shockwaves of pleasure rippling through my body. Your hands roam over me with a hunger that knows no bounds, tracing the contours of my body with a reverence that leaves me breathless.

With each caress, I can feel the tension building between us, a coiling spring of desire that threatens to snap at any moment. Our bodies move together in a primal rhythm, slick with sweat and fueled by an insatiable need for each other.

The tangy scent of our mingled sweat fills the air, intoxicating and heady, as our skin becomes slick with the heat of our passion. It's a symphony of sensation, each touch leaving a searing imprint on my skin that I know will linger long after the night is over.

In this moment, there's no room for anything but the urgent, feverish need to consume and be consumed by each other. I am yours, completely and utterly, lost in the raw, unbridled intensity of our connection. And in your embrace, I find my salvation, my sanctuary from the chaos of the world outside.

45 ▌

Broken Walls

In the realm of our connection, aspirations and shared dreams were visible through delicate glass walls. However, my stubbornness constructed an impenetrable fortress, reluctant to let you traverse the corridors of my vulnerabilities. Undeterred, you persistently chipped away at the transparent barrier, each crack a testament to your unwavering determination.

As the glass finally shattered, so did the stronghold of my stubbornness. The shards scattered like fallen barriers, leaving the path open for you to navigate the intricacies of my heart. Your hugs, once on the other side of that transparent divide, transformed into a refuge of warmth, wrapping me in the reassurance of your embrace.

Your kisses, like a masterful conductor, wielded a magical control over me. With each tender touch of your lips, my defenses crumbled, and the orchestration of our connection reached symphonic heights. It was in those stolen moments, where the power of your kiss became an undeniable force, unraveling the threads of my resistance.

Even in the tempest of our arguments, our conflicts were not mere storms; they were explosive, yet strangely beautiful. Amid the thunderous clashes, I remained tethered to you, and you to me. The heat of our disagreements forged an unbreakable bond, where even in our most heated moments, the undeniable truth echoed: I was yours, and you were undeniably mine.

46

Desires

I hunger for you, crave you in a way that consumes my very soul. Your skin against mine is a wildfire, a frenzy of heat and desire that scorches every inch of my being. I ache to claim you as mine with a ferocity that leaves no room for doubt or hesitation.

From the moment our eyes locked, I was ensnared by a primal force that demands our union. The universe itself seems to conspire, urging us to surrender to the tempestuous passion that binds us together. And when our bodies collide, it's as if lightning strikes, electrifying every nerve with a searing intensity that defies reason.

Your touch is like a drug, intoxicating and addictive, sending shockwaves of pleasure crashing through me. I hunger for the taste of your lips, the feel of your skin beneath my fingertips, as if I could engulf you whole and still crave more.

I yearn to explore every hidden corner of your being, to delve into the depths of your desires and lose myself in the ecstasy of our connection. I want to immerse myself in you utterly, to mark you with the essence of my passion so that no other could ever lay claim to my heart.

But beyond the physical, I long to intertwine our souls, to become one in mind, body, and spirit. I want to be your anchor in the storm, the refuge you seek in moments of chaos and uncertainty. Together, we will forge a bond that transcends time and space, a love that burns brighter than the stars themselves.

So let me devour you, let me consume you until there is nothing left but us, bound together in a blaze of unquenchable desire. Let me make you mine, completely and irrevocably, for now and for all eternity.

47

Heart

Within the fortress of your chest, lies a kingdom of secrets, guarded by the sentinels of your ribs. Your heart, a silent monarch, reigns over this domain with a quiet authority, its throne room echoing with the whispers of forgotten dreams and unspoken desires.

Each beat is a proclamation, a declaration of sovereignty over the realm of your emotions. It pulses with the rhythm of ancient drums, resonating through the corridors of your soul like a haunting melody.

Within its chambers, the flames of passion flicker and dance, casting shadows upon the walls like ghostly apparitions. It is a sanctuary of yearning, where the echoes of past loves and lost dreams linger like echoes in the night.

But amidst the darkness, there lies a beacon of light, a flickering flame of hope that refuses to be extinguished. It is the heart's eternal flame, a testament to the resilience of the human spirit and the enduring power of kindness.

Within its depths, lies the key to unlocking the mysteries of the universe, a doorway to realms unseen and dreams unspoken. It is a font of boundless creativity, fuelling the fires of inspiration and igniting the flames of passion.

And in its infinite capacity for compassion, it offers solace to the weary traveller, a sanctuary where wounds are healed and sorrows are soothed. It is the heartbeat of humanity, a pulsing reminder of our shared connection to one another and to the world around us.

So, let your heart be your guide, a compass in the vast expanse of existence, leading you towards the shores of understanding and the embrace of empathy. For within its depths lies the true essence of who you are, a beacon of light in the darkness, a sanctuary of hope in a world of uncertainty.

48

The reality

Oh, dear reader, how cruelly hope has ensnared you in its treacherous web.

You've journeyed through these pages, clutching your heart with the desperate belief that redemption was within reach, that love could pull this tortured soul from the abyss. But hope, that insidious, fragile light, has done nothing but blind you to the darkness that has always been there, lurking in every shadow of this tragic tale.

From the first words, a warning whispered through the ink—a foreboding that this path was never meant to lead to happiness. Yet you pressed on, eyes wide with the fervent belief that perhaps, just perhaps, this story would defy its own prophecy. You clung to the possibility of a miracle, your faith unshaken by the encroaching night.

But oh, how that belief has only deepened the wound that now festers in your soul.

The protagonist you followed, the one whose pain you shared, whose desperate grasp for sanity you witnessed—he was already lost before you ever found him. He had slipped into the chasm of his own mind long before you joined him on this harrowing journey. The madness that consumed him was no mere passing shadow but a voracious force that hollowed him out, leaving behind only a grotesque shell of what once was.

Imagine, if you dare, the horrifying tableau that now remains. His body, once a vessel of fragile hope and longing, now lies in a grotesque sprawl upon the cold, unforgiving floor. His once-animated eyes have sunken deep into their sockets, staring vacantly with a lifeless glaze that reflects only the bleakness of eternity. The skin, now pallid and stretched tight over bone, is marred by a sickening pallor, discoloured and mottled as though the very essence of vitality has been drained from it. Flies buzz lazily around the festering wounds, a grotesque testament to the decay that has taken hold.

His mind, once a battleground of fleeting sanity, has rotted into an abyss of darkness. The torment he suffered has left an indelible mark—a gaping void where thought and reason once resided. What remains is an insidious rot, a putrid stench of despair that permeates the very air around him. His thoughts, once sharp and fleeting, have dissolved into an unholy mire of madness, leaving behind only a festering pit of anguish and sorrow.

The soul, that elusive essence of being, has been consumed by a ravenous darkness. It seeps from every pore of his decaying form, a vile substance of blackened despair mingling with the pool of blood that surrounds him. The blood, now congealed and darkened, forms a grotesque halo around his corpse, a macabre testament to the final, fatal plunge into the abyss of his own mind.

Did you not see the signs, reader? The moments when reality fractured, when the darkness seemed too thick to ever part? Those were not mere obstacles on a path to healing—they were the very truth of his existence. He was drowning in the depths of his own mind, and each step he took was not toward the light, but deeper into the void.

And what of the love you so desperately wished for him? The love that seemed to promise salvation, a hand reaching through the darkness to pull him back into the light? It was nothing more than a cruel illusion, a fleeting dream conjured by a dying mind grasping at the remnants of hope. That love was not real, reader—it was a phantom, a haunting echo of a life he could never grasp, a happiness forever out of reach.

You were led to believe in a recovery that was never possible, in a salvation that was nothing but a mirage. The protagonist did not find peace; he did not find love. He perished, alone and unseen, lost in the prison of his own making, yet you remained oblivious to his own death . Dear reader, were left to wander through the ruins of his mind, searching for a glimmer of hope that never truly existed.

There is no solace here, no comforting resolution to ease the ache that now grips your heart. The tragedy lies not just in the protagonist's fate but in your own—for you, too, were ensnared in the web of false promises and shattered dreams. You were made to feel his despair, to grasp at his hope, only to have it wrenched away as the truth came crashing down.

The protagonist's death was not a singular moment, not a scene laid bare before your eyes—it was a gradual, insidious descent that you, in your hope, mistook for survival. He had already faded into the abyss, leaving behind only the faintest echoes of what might have been.

Now, as you close this book, you are left with the crushing weight of that realization, the unbearable sorrow of understanding the depths of his despair. You were warned, from the very beginning, that this was never meant to be a story of redemption. And yet, you allowed yourself to believe otherwise.

So here you stand, at the end of this harrowing journey, with nothing but the echoes of a shattered heart and the lingering cries of a mind that was lost long ago. The protagonist is gone, and with him, all the hopes and dreams you dared to harbour have turned to ashes.

Dear reader, you have shared in his tragedy, and now you must carry the weight of this sorrow alone. This is the final, inescapable truth: There was never a happy ending, only the grotesque remains of a soul twisted by despair, the haunting echoes of what might have been, and the relentless ache of dreams forever denied.

Close the book and let it drift into the quiet shadows, for within its pages lies only a phantom—a flickering mirage of a love that never truly breathed. What you have glimpsed is not a tale of earnest affection but a mirage dancing on the edge of a desolate void. The longing inscribed here is a mournful echo from a heart that reached for ethereal stars, only to clutch at the darkened abyss.

This narrative is not the saga of a life fully lived but a tragic descent into a maze of madness. The relentless cries of his shattered mind reverberate like a lost soul adrift in a tempest, spiralling towards an inevitable chasm. His end was not merely a conclusion but a silent capitulation to the shadows that had long ensnared him.

Let the book fall into the silence, and allow the quiet to embrace you. The love depicted was a fleeting spectre, conjured by the desperate whispers of a soul unravelling in darkness. The true tragedy is not the love that remained forever just out of reach but the slow disintegration of a mind devoured by its own nightmarish despair. For this indeed is a tragedy. From the outset, you were warned that no happy ending awaited. He implored, "Don't linger on my account. Don't wait for me. This is not a story with a triumphant climax. I fear I am headed to an unwanted destination, so don't wait for me."

Yet, despite the forewarnings and the omens that danced like shadows on the periphery, you lingered. You waited, entangled in the delicate web of his unravelling, bearing silent witness to the quiet descent that unfolded like a darkening storm. In the hushed silence that now surrounds you, grasp the truth: you were not merely a spectator but a ghostly observer of his final unravelling. The end that had been foretold—an inevitable plunge into the void—came to pass, even as you remained ensnared by the illusion of hope. In the stillness, recognize the profound reality that you witnessed not just the conclusion, but the slow dissolution of a soul lost in its own shadowy abyss, an end you had been cautioned about, yet could not escape.

This narrative is not the saga of a life fully lived, but a tragic descent into a maze of madness. His shattered mind cried out in agony, lost like a ghost adrift in a storm, spiralling towards an inevitable chasm. His madness had left him blurring the lines between reality and hallucination, creating a world where truth and illusion became one. His end was not a peaceful conclusion but a silent surrender to the shadows that had long claimed him.

Let the book fall into the silence, and let the quiet embrace you. The love depicted was nothing more than a fleeting ghost, conjured by the desperate whispers of a soul unravelling in the dark. The true tragedy is not the love that remained forever out of reach, but the slow, agonizing disintegration of a mind devoured by its own nightmarish despair.

And still, despite the forewarnings, despite the omens that fluttered like dying embers, you lingered. You waited, entwined in the fragile web of his unravelling, a silent witness to the quiet descent that crept upon you like a suffocating shadow. And now, as the final words dissolve into nothingness, you too must retrace your steps, for the journey does not end here. In the hushed silence that now surrounds you, grasp the unbearable truth: you were not merely a spectator, but a companion to his final unravelling. The end that had been foretold—his inevitable plunge into the void—came to pass, even as you clung to the fragile illusion of hope.

In the stillness, as the weight of what you've read settles like a stone in your chest, recognize the tragic reality that you have borne witness to not just an ending, but the slow, excruciating dissolution of a soul consumed by its own torment. And now, the lingering, heart-wrenching question is left to you—what was real, and what was merely a reflection of what could have been? The truth lies buried in the shadows of his fractured mind, and it is you who must now sift through the wreckage, to decide where reality ends and the haunting echoes of his madness begin.

Amaan Shabir is a multifaceted author known for his thought-provoking exploration of themes such as love, mental health, power dynamics, and societal norms. His literary works often blur the lines between reality and metaphor, inviting readers to delve into the depths of the human psyche and confront uncomfortable truths about the world around them.

Amaan's debut novel, "Scarred Visions," serves as a poignant reflection of his own experiences with mental health, friendship and betrayal. Set within the metaphorical city of Ashways, the novel follows the journey of a protagonist navigating the highs and lows of mania and depression while grappling with the complexities of relationships and personal identity.

In his follow-up novel, "Unveiled Concealment," he delves into themes of self-acceptance and the transformative power of love. Through the metaphorical city of Fleshborne, readers are invited to explore the beauty of embracing one's flaws and vulnerabilities, challenging societal expectations and norms along the way.

Shabir's writing style is characterized by its innovative and unconventional approach, often blending narrative storytelling with poetry, autobiographical elements, and dystopian metaphors. His works resonate with readers of all ages, offering a compelling blend of introspection, emotion, and social commentary.

Beyond his literary endeavors, Shabir is also known for his influence as a social media figure and fashion collaborator. However, in recent years, he has shifted his focus towards promoting his writing and raising awareness about mental health issues, using his platform to advocate for greater understanding and empathy.

Overall, Amaan Shabir's works stand as a testament to the power of storytelling to illuminate the human experience and provoke meaningful dialogue about the challenges and triumphs we encounter along life's journey. Through his unique blend of creativity, insight, and vulnerability, Shabir continues to captivate readers and inspire reflection long after the final page is turned.